Sleeveless

Sleeveless

a novel by

Joi Brozek

Phony Lid Books

LOS ANGELES · 2002

Acknowledgments: First and foremost, thank you to Steve Fried of Lunar Offensive Press for giving me my first real publishing credit, not to mention a hell of a lot of creative inspiration. Kelly Dessaint and Jesse Hopkins, thank you for all of your hard work and support throughout and becoming my good friends, as well. Eve Rings—it's all about six degrees of Eve, don't you know? Eric Britto, your hard work, love and support have helped me come to this. Thanks also to the following people: Mom and Dad, Jason Brozek, Hubert Selby, Jr., Jerry Stahl, Allison Barker, Susie Hu, Tom Piccarilli, Nick Mamatas, Greg Gifune, Mike Halchin, Robert Pepper, Mike McPadden, Chris Blooddoll Bevard, Melissa Rose, Raugust, and Roberta Solomon.

Portions of this book have previously appeared in *Rag Shock*, *Cthulu Sex*, *Driver's Side Airbag* and in the chapbook, *Blood and a Windshield Make Lovely Stained Glass*, published by Lunar Offensive Press.

PHONY LID BOOKS
PoBox 29066
Los Angeles, Ca 90029

ISBN: 1-930935-26-9

Library of Congress Control Number: 2001094566

FIRST EDITION

Phony Lid Books are edited and designed by Kelly Dessaint and Jesse Hopkins.

For my great grandmother,
I live here, where you left.

Prelude: Fist

MY SISTER IS PREGNANT. *Fucked*, I say. You're so *fucked*. Was, she answers, with a touch of irony. She just thinks of it as cells forming, but I tell her it's a nascent fist that's going to punch the hell out of her on the way out and then resent her for its life. It'll claw her for giving birth to it, I just know it. She believes me because I'm older. We might have been twins, we might have been separated by several years, it's all no matter, really. What we have is love.

My mother lost her mind like she lost her faith. She had almost become a full-fledged nun. Until she was fucked. Erasing her sins and ensuring that we would never be tempted became her life's mission, instead. She is actually more a contemporary of the bible variety sinner than the classic martyr, so she might as well lose the baby shrine.

That day I had the flu. Jenny fiddled for hours with the hanger in the closet. Ease of pain was an issue, of course. I was snorting silly and my throat was full and forced a salty mouthful of mucus on my tongue whether I liked it or not. I was born in such mucus. A bare light bulb gave the closet a nightclub feel. Especially when I flicked the light on and off to ease the anxiety out of Jenny. Unfortunately, it reminded her too much of the conception. Maybe the strobe effect caused her to have a sort of seizure. I don't know. There was thrashing and I felt like I was at a show with a private viewing. Should I have watched? Shouldn't it have been a private something? I invaded. She looked graceful and determined, yet miserable at the same time. I wanted to be involved. I wanted to make her smile at least. I reminded her of our happy times in the garden, and slowly but surely, the fist became a flower.

So, I discovered a jacket. *Her* jacket. There was a pocket. Inside, I discovered her intentions. Pocket full of fuzzy, gummy pennies, girly-girl bowed barrettes (pink and yellow), and there, in gracious script, "safe"...proclamations! Guarantees! All outlined on innocuous flyer. Safe, private, safe, *real* doctors, women! There was the curious odor of it all around, though, the odor of meat. And money. All in a pocket, full.

D.I.Y. was *your* suggestion, *Dear Heart*. Your cheap, kingly suggestion, *My Love*.

My baby sister Jenny and I are in a bathtub of pink sailboats. I'm older, so I teach her the chant. When we get out, I decide to go vegetarian. Meat—I never could stomach the sight of it. It's all about the bread. The bread that must never be turned over the wrong way, because God will cry, our mother always told us.

It was Christmas. X-Mass. Silent night, holy night, all is calm, all is blight, 'round young...we wouldn't have a Baby New Year after all. How many times did I tell her. Dreams, no such thing. Nightmares reigned supreme in our fairyland. The closet.

I'm a vegetarian. I can't do this. Take care of your own problems, your meaty situations. I don't give head anymore. You understand, *Dear Heart*. Changing oneself is all a part of growing up, we're told. Also, it's a sin to swallow, surely it is.

Smoking cloves was my way of stunting my growth. One a day for a year, cancer guaranteed. I got off on that. That and the sweetness on my lips. That and the autumn scented smoke. That and the way the end burnt so cleanly into my skin. That and the way you'd get an instantaneous hard-on.

I want to help Jenny. I love her like candy. But the sight of it; I need it to be *pretty* to deal. That's how our mother, our Nunny, raised us. Being pretty, in the soft *pink* room. Oh sunny, like cherry. I want to bite Jenny. Nunny would *die* if she knew my childhood fantasies of poking my finger in my baby sister's fontanel. Cleanliness next to Godliness, bread facing up to God and doing unto others as they would do unto you. I'm all about that. All of that.

Slit slash making a rash, merrily training down the tracks, with the countryside so like my skin. Hissing cows and howling birds welcome all road diseases. The pernicious southern sun mingles with the newly made road map. The molasses from that tree is sticky, too. You bled the tree, darling. Just like now, you're bleeding me. A cemetery just sang by, all full of ancient bathtubs and spires. Anxious to see you, despite the rash I hide disguised by sweet molasses. I wait, despite. Don't break my neck, precious. Or the tree. *Dear Heart*.

Jenny, I asked, where exactly would we *put* the thing? How would we clean up? Cleanliness is next to Godliness, Nunny would say. Such a thing, so meaty. So filthy. Be an angel, a dear dear *angel*, and come to me.

I miss the days of Jenny and roses. Jenny and I would play outside in the muddy garden, surrounded by green vines and red roses. She believed I was giving her chocolate milk in a pail, in the muddy garden. Jenny-blood-and-roses. I was her savior once.

Poking, toking, we shared so much, my love. You shared my poking fantasies of my sister. You acted on them, *Dear Heart*. Fontanel. Slit. Same meaty difference—just on opposite ends.

My bowed barrettes. *My* Donny and Marie dolls. *My* fashion plates. *My* Dexy's Midnight Runners record. *My* pink fishnet tights. *My* artwork. *My* bad habits. *My* catastrophes. *My* true love. *My* boyfriend. *My* little sister. But *her* fist.

We grew up good Catholics, Nunny, Jenny and I. Sunday Mass made us honking geese in the flock. Devout as *hell*, we were. I enjoyed it there and hung out in confession often. She always made me go, but secretly I enjoyed it. All good Catholic children attend confession regularly as soon as one's Penance is made. That is what we were.

Passing her hand, pressing over the budding garden of burden, she was crushing it into mulch with that punishing young hand. Cotton candy froth dreams were dreaming in her head, flower quietly feeding in her womb. She was bursting not to bloom. Then she curled up into her own and wondered about the petaled embryo longing to be let out.

I called you *precious* and *darling*; both are words I detest. Together we conspired. Right before this all happened. You, *Dear Heart*, and I, it was you and I. There and then I fucked and bled. Bleeding, carving, fucking all into a pretty collage of severed heads and rag dolls. Then you did this to me. And you, my strong sweet treat, bled me like a tree. Don't pity me like Jenny's fist. *Your* fist, too. But blood is thicker than man's bitter life-giving fluids. Jenny is blood.

Our mother was almost a nun who got the fist and fled. She knew she could never return and face the rake. So she stayed as religious as ever, but gave up nundom and had me. Then she got fucked again and had another. You'd think she'd have learned about the threat of the light bulb after the first time. And now, there is a shrine to the lost baby. It's on the kitchen table, with Catholic Saint trading cards surrounding a few candles.

The bathtub is full of warm, flowery foam. Jenny and I are across from each other, twats mere inches away. I feel hers *breathe* on mine. She smiles and I see if the pink sailboat can fit in hers. I try to be gentle while putting it inside. She's curious and wincing at the same time. *It won't go*, she sobs. *You're bigger so try yours*. So I do and I only get the tip in and then our mother comes barging in like God.

She took the hanger and bent it into a long, long stem, weapon on the end, and it gleamed like a copper rake under the bare light bulb, burning her back from above. And she lit the flame and let it lick the hooked end which she took—no mercy on herself, *no no NO Mercy*—and put inside. Skinny cold metal burned her thighs.

I'm on my way to see you now, precious punch. *Dear Heart.* I bring news and sighting of your fist, finished and covered with third degree burns from the bare bulb in the closet. Your fist, so like you, so angry. Like father, like fist.

Jenny grabs my hand in the tub and rubs her pudgy belly with it. We're wiggling giggly fish in the sudsy water. She won't let me make pink ribbons of my flesh with Nunny's razor on the edge of the tub, even though I tell her it'll be pretty. I'll love her forever, I tell her. Such a long time ago.

I looked at my arms today. Scars white on my yellow skin. Eggs, scrambled, no red left to indicate blood bubbles. *Who's the most beautiful girl in the world?* I don't need to wonder. *You are, you are,* our Nunny would tell us alternately. *Snow White, piss yellow, egg skinned girl, a princess with the grace of God.*

The rake yanked it from the garden and it came out rather reluctantly from the warmth, a puckered face (the small rose fist), attached to a never ending stem, looking furious about dying.

The lights flicker. I crouch in the corner of the room

singing something by Patsy Cline. Someone tells me to stop fingering myself. *Why?* I think, it's not public here. Where are you, *Precious?* I can't wait to rub your sticky burned offspring in your face. I am no longer crouching.

I am being crucified for it. *I didn't mean it,* I think, I beg. I didn't I didn't I didn't. *Sin, what a sin,* they all whispered. Nunny was sitting bent over, like a hanger. It's odd, it may even be wrong. She always held sin over my head. Why isn't she doing that now? *My fault?* It is certainly my fault.

Jenny and I are in the garden. I'm making pies of sweet mud with *my* yellow shovel made of plastic. Jenny's shovel is pink. She looks starved and so I offer her some chocolate milk, an ingredient for my pie. She drinks it and vomits right away. Brown for the mud. Blood for the roses.

And glitter rained from the garden of ruin and she looked on at the dead blossom, overjoyed. I picked it up, intrigued by how sticky and gummy it was. Startled by its minute fluttering against my fingers, I dropped it. It never lost its fury even after it finally died mere seconds later by the hard light of life in the closet. And I saw my sister's face like a perfect mother-of-pearl now, smooth from relief, red from forcing it out. *He forced me,* she told me, finally. *Don't worry,* I told her, burning the fist in the closet.

one: Losing

SUMMER/EARLY FALL 1988

All times happen at once.
Fast forward. Stop.
Rewind...my mind, my mind...
It was all real.

Singeing on Independence Day

I REMEMBER WHEN JENNY TOLD ME, how she told me. That day...funny how the memory twists like the structure of DNA. Helix day.

Our mother, our *Nunny*, the bright as *atomic flash* woman, planned a barbecue for the Fourth of July with all of our "friends and family," and I "fucked things up." She didn't understand my intentions, but then she never does, never did and never will. All she understood was that her pristine reputation was ruined. That and her hairdo.

All I wanted to do was help. This was my sister, after all, the *most important* person in my life. I could also have accomplished more with my action if it was implemented correctly, which it wasn't. Everything was blown out of proportion. Nunny just invited the wrong people. Church fanatics and Philistines of the trailer park variety.

I, Lisha Lady Fingers—just "Fingers" to you, man— I see my heaven-in-waiting at a corner fruit stand. I'm gonna Crash! *my music into charity. I'm eyeing the watermelons which I will see* Crack-Bash-Boom! *into fiery spheres with cherry bombs, M-80s, ashcans, bottle rockets, jumping jacks, here.* Zoom! *The fruit of the sky and I buy five huge twenty pounders, yeah. No one will go hungry, no, not even the flounders. Into the bag they all go. I drag it like a huge sea otter; I drag it to my happy house on the bay, a warm, warm place; an obnox-*

ious holiday, soon to get even hotter. It's July Four. I wait for dark and the screaming song I will feed—no pour! *to the fishies who dread sushi thoughts but will get fed with the raining of airborne fruit instead. I, Lady Fingers*—ka ching!

I told Nunny, oh Holy One, that I would be providing the entertainment for the evening. I'd put on a spectacle to blow peoples' minds.

"A puppet show on the deck for the children?" she asked.

"Nah, something even better. It'll be a surprise, you'll see," I said, not really even knowing yet.

A benevolent display of sparklers sticking up from the dirt all over the backyard in the shape of a cross was my *initial* plan. Then Jenny, my sister, dropped this head trip on me, which definitely altered my cheery mood. However, I had to give her credit for inspiring a creative idea for the day. Ever heard the expression, "with fruit?"

"Lisha," she wailed, "what the hell am I going to do about it? I'm only fifteen!"

"Watch my show later tonight," I said. "I'll think of something. The message will be there for you to figure out yourself. It shouldn't be too hard."

I didn't know at that moment what I was going to do yet, but I was definitely excited enough to trash my silly sparkler plan. Her news could have really done a number on me. But I channeled my initial shock into creative inspiration.

I, Lady Fingers, I finger my pride, while fantasizing 'bout treating my melons with M-80s. I don't slouch man, nah I glide through them streets singing—not shouting, Crash! Bam! Boom!

Like I said, Jenny really had me bumming and when I get depressed I usually crash, expecting to find myself in my dreams. It was around noon or so and too sunny to even think about sleeping, so I pulled down my dark red shades and lit my black bulb for a three hour nap. First I dreamt about an orchestra. The conductor waved a lit punk stick and all of this fruit exploded when he waved it at them.

Next, I had an *Easter* nightmare. God, I hate Easter. It's such a vapid celebration. And all that pastel shit, flowers and various candies shaped like the poor animals people would eat that day. In this dream, tulips (the tampon applicator flowers) were growing gonads into gardens. And lavender bunnies and green chicks were coming at me from all angles like starving rats. These animals were skin, color and bones. I was desperate, so I threw fish which magically appeared in my hands at them, and this was the worst part—I perverted vegetarian animals! They were so starved that they ate the fish and I didn't even think, the *I* in the dream that is, that I was fucking up these animals because I was so eager to save my own ass. I awoke, feeling guilty with a new type of anxiety. *I really had to help my sister.* I finally realized how I could. She'd never want to add to our already fucked up menagerie of a family.

And I see Mr. Policeman. Jumping Jack. He says— he knows me—he says, "Hey Lady. Hey Fingers. Where's your holiday? Where's the party at? Gonna lay out? Gonna get a tan from the moon?" So I say back, "Hey Jumping Jack! Where's the crime at? Gonna bust me? I'm legal. I'm with fruit. Party at eight 'round. Gonna make your eyes pop like cannons with sight and sound.

And good nutrition. Gonna finger feed them fishies!"
And I'm so outta there. I win! Never scared. He loves me,
who doesn't? I, Lady Fingers—Ka ching!

Connections will get you everywhere. I purchased
the sparklers from this kid at school. He went into Chi-
natown every year and got some good deals on fireworks. He would give me a good price, I thought. He
owed me one, let's just say. "Lisha, all I got left are
some M-80s. No roman candles or any fancy shit." I told
him for my purposes all I needed were the bombs, the
explosives. "We're supposed to be artists—make our
own displays," I reminded him. He, of course, felt stupid
and agreed immediately. Fuck mediocrity. I didn't want
him to think this was my *sole* artistic outlet or anything, but I always like to go that extra hundred miles.
I could see the M-80s exploding the fruit into lush fragrant volcanoes.

I, Lady Fingers. I'm almost home, yeah, psyched to
the bone. Psyched to the sounds in my head, Crash!
Bam! Boom! *That sonata in waiting, that sonata of fire-*
works and fruit. I'm zooming, zooming like a rocket,
dragging my loot.

When the party was in full force, I came out of my
house to my backyard where I passed the lighters and
sparklers to the little ones; no need to get them hurt
with dangerous stuff. I remember how I used to light
fireworks myself when I was their age, with no officious
adults creating a nuisance with their help. So I gave
them lighters, safer than matches, in my book, and let
them have at it.

There were hordes of neighbors huddled like lepers
around Christ, but in reality around the Almighty
Hibachi, waiting for charred chow. "I want mine black

and blue," I heard this chick from around the corner announce to my mother. Intrigued by the prospect of beef with bruises, I approached the crowd and asked, "What the fuck does that mean?"

"That's burnt on the outside, rare on the inside," I was informed by the drooling woman.

"Oh," I answered. "Don't you mean to call that *cancer and worms?*" I could see Nunny was far from amused, so I went to start my project.

And I see old Mr. Zoo. I see him hobble towards me, so I leap to a stop. And he says—he knows me—he says, "Hey Lady. Hey Fingers. What's your music this time? What's your scene? What's that huge bag of watermelon mean?" So I say back, "That's MS. Fingers to you, Zoo. Don't disrespect me, I conduct a symphony and a masterpiece above the sea. Come eight 'round. Gonna make your eyes pop like cannons with sight and sound." And the old dude grins his face into a fuzzy kiwi chin grin. Bless him, I, Lady Fingers—Ka ching!

I took a medium sized melon, twenty pounds or so, from a sack I had dragged from the garage to the deck, and started to dig holes through the rind. The adults, intent on their feast, didn't notice my preparation. But of course the children, finished with the sparklers now, gathered around me to watch. I methodically did the same with the other four melons. I sucked on the tunnels of watery pulp like skin tissue while I placed the little rockets, two per melon, on opposite sides as far in as possible, but not next to one another. I left the fuses sticking out on both ends and carefully put them back in the sack to wait for later.

Bomb! Bash! Boom! *And I think of how happy the fish are gonna be soon. And them watermelons, I'm gonna lambast them bombs-as-pits, flesh and rind.*

The sun went down at around 9 p.m. By now the gluttons were reclining in their chairs, satisfied with the spread they had inhaled for free. I made my announcement, "Folks, direct your focus to the bay, please."

In front of my house now and I see Ms. Reba Cycle coming at me from behind. She's spying my bag. She says—she knows me—she says, "Hey Lady. Hey Ms. Fingers. What about the fish? Just where are they going to go?" So I say back, "Don't you know, Ms. Cycle? Their palates are gonna rule and roar smack! *My little fishies are gonna sing with the cantata." She thinks about it— she's sedated, satisfied with the meal I've created of fresh watermelons seething with vitamins. I, Lady Fingers.* Kaching! *Good Samaritan.*

It really took some coaxing to get them away from gorging on the dessert spread, just now produced by Nunny. I rushed over to my charlatan mother. "Nunny, for God's sake, I think *now* is the time to start the entertainment."

"Oh, honey, we're eating dessert. Can't it wait until later?"

"No, actually, it can't. I may just lose the momentum. The show must go on—and *now*. It's for Jenny. She desperately needs my help. Do you want *that* on your conscience?"

She turned back without another word to her precious tiramisu. I could see bloody raspberry sauce drizzle over the top, and it seemed to be a wound covering the marzipan icing. Like Nunny's hair drizzled from her head, as tempting as any *dessert* ever could be to me. She really pissed me off right then and there. I couldn't wait to make her pay attention.

Jack, Cycle, Zoo, hundreds of others, their children too, are in my backyard surrounding me. I say—they know me, they adore me, they worship me—I say, "Hey, welcome to my show. Keep those eyes pinned to the sky and bay, here I go!" Bomb-bast *it all!*

"Nunny!" I screamed like I meant it this time.

"Lisha," she started threateningly, but never finished the insult. I took the watermelon, the fuses lit on either end, and tossed it in her general direction.

All at once, a rocket zoomed—like a baby on speed—out of the melon, narrowly missing her face, but doing a good job on her hairdo. I heard the gasps of gorged lepers. I saw Jenny's look of recognition as the flesh of the melon was dripping on the side of the garage like an afterbirth. Everything was sticky in the backyard. Nunny looked like she had made a quick excursion into a microwave, but came out not too much worse for the wear. I think she was more embarrassed than anything else, what with all her friends and brethren gathered 'round her.

I, Lady-licking-Fingers, Bomb! *I sing to the sky, I see kiddees around me, all with crusades in their eyes. They want fun—they don't want to lose. I take an explosive-gorged melon in my hand and kiss my punk to the fuse. I launch it for the sky to catch—now here's my surprise.* Crash—Bomb—Flash! *I, the wizard with gunpowder as my potion, the adults come running, puzzled about the commotion. Before the feast has sunk to the starfish, I offer another and another and I see Nunny, and to her I sing, "Got a hot dish!"* I, Lady Fingers—Ka ching!

There was this idiot pig at the barbecue. One in every crowd, motherfucker. Before I could toast him with explosives he got things happening fast. Before I was able to touch the lighter to the second watermelon, before I could wash my hands of sticky juice and gunpowder, before the smell of singed hair dissipated from the back yard, a patrol car wailed its way into my driveway and this neophyte had me in the cuffs. He should have just been more meat for the Hibachi to char, but no such luck. I looked at Jenny. She was tending to Nunny's singed hairdo. I wondered if she could now see what one's offspring was capable of doing. Most of Mom's friends were huddled by the garage, watching the whole spectacle; gloating, patting their own safe bouffants.

I see the people smiling, I see adoration, I see concern for the fish. My mother is so proud. I want to grab her, I want to sing out loud, "I Lady—Savior To The Hungry Fish—Fingers, I'm so glad you care. To the rest, I would love to share." So I turn back to the masses and make an offer of fruit. To everyone, sincerity and melon I bring, I Lady Fingers—Ka ching!

Those fucking porkers didn't know squat about my family. Without my help, Jenny would just be adding another fruit to the family. That Mom had to pay a small price that her beautician would be more than happy to fix was the icing on the tiramisu.

But this was the grossest part. The pig with the largest donut gut said to my mother, "I'll talk to her, ma'am," and brought me to the side of the shed. He thought he was so fucking cool. "God bless Officer Bob," I could hear Nunny saying.

I-95, or Vacation of Cruelty

Road stop on the New Jersey Turnpike

Bathroom as crowded as a factory farm. Over *this* goddess' head, a nimbus of wet brown paper towels, hair spray, meaty-smelling shit, perfume, tampons and coffee piss. Think back to when Nunny drove us to see our relatives in South Carolina and I made her stop at road stops every half hour under the threat of pissing on the car seat, but really 'cause I wanted to glimpse some road culture. And get away from her. Bored and turned off by crowds of High-Mai Gals primping and fucking their reflections in the mirrors, I exit the bathroom and find myself in the midst of Convenience Wonderland. Roy Rogers. TCBY. Big Boy. Magazine store with Jackie Collins and Stephen King paperbacks too. Souvenir stand (souvenirs of Jersey?) selling useful things like pewter baby spoons with the Garden State on the end. They've got it all in these places. Giant gum ball dispenser as soon as you walk in the doors. Children in pastel shorts running like they've been freed from Hell, something like the backseat of their parents' cars, maybe. Portly parents clutching food stuff—Dads with greasy bags of Kentucky Fried Chicken and Icees. Moms with large styrofoam cups of milky coffee and melted fat-free frozen yogurt, baiting their children with promises of fuel. No dice. Then comes the blackmail. "If you don't get over here right now, you little shit, we're just gonna turn back home and you can forget about Disneyworld. GET OVER HERE!" This, when the kiddies call their bluff. All this in an instant, on the quick path from the bathroom, and Billy heading over to get his caffeine fix. Only twenty more hours until we get *there*. I grab an issue of *Cosmo* to laugh at in the car. I'll play with those model faces, like poke the eyes out and stick in little pins for facial jewelry and recolor the hair and make-up, behead them. Then I'll tape a few pretty heads to the dashboard. They could be our trophies. Or good luck charms, even. Maybe in a few hours I can add real blood (if Billy is nice, that is) to ooze out from the cuts on their faces. Blood makes beauty. Hey, I can dream.

Back on the Turnpike:

"Hey Lish, did you see that little kid who lit his *cotton candy* on fire? It seemed like a bush fire or something."

"Uh, no. I was too busy grabbing that guy's food for you, *Dear Heart*, at just the right moment when he went to go get some ketchup. The least you could do is give me some fries; they're the only thing I can eat from that slaughter stand."

"Yes! I love me slaughter, fetch me some more later, my buxom serving wench. Owwww…what the fuck, Lish? Go read a fucking book if you can't take a joke. You know I hate it when I'm not prepared for this shit. At least prepare me."

"Tough. Half the fun is in the surprise. Listen, don't talk to me for a while. I must concentrate on the task at hand while it's still light."

"Oh goody. *Cosmo*."

Three hours later, Maryland Welcome Center

A beautiful walk from the parking lot to the Welcome Center. Some people even notice the numerous trickles of dried blood running down Billy's arm, and ask if everything is okay and I smile my precious girl smile and say nothing. Sure, it might disconcert them, disturb their smiling sunshine day, but who cares? Once inside, we look in each other's eyes and kiss passionately, tongues in full view by youngsters and oldsters alike. Sounds of teeth gnashing, tsks and giggles. His blood, gun metal warm. Our malodorous breath intermingles and our mouths become one shared tomb to our teeth and tongues. We, like the others, are hungry too. We realize it at the same time. Break apart and head for food court. Find mushy spaghetti strands glued to each other by bland coppery sauce. Inhale it down my throat anyway. Sit next to each other at a table. Never stop holding hands. Dig my sharp nails in his palm. Draw blood and realize he has a hard-on. Was it the blood? Discreetly pull down his zipper, not many can see behind the table, and massage his prick. Take some blood from his palm and dab a bit on it. Prick pricked. He doesn't appreciate blood there, but right now he doesn't notice it. Probably thinks it's lube or something. He gets off and we leave. Glares from folks who don't know how to appreciate love. I bop away, all girly like, and my skirt is so short it goes up and then the men stop glaring and start gaping.

I-95 Maryland somewhere:

"Aw, Lisha come *on*."

"Absolutely not, man. Like, you're driving, okay?"

"Oh there's enough room for your head over here."

"Like that's what I'm worried about."

"Then what?"

"Like an *accident*, okay? I'm not about to be the next item on the Road Kill Cafe's menu. Are you nuts? Ouch, sorry. I hate puns."

"Fuck! First you tease me with that kiss in there, and then after we get our food, I think you're gonna make good on your promise and you stop in the middle and drag me back to the car..."

"Hey, okay, I thought you got *off*, okay? We can't fool around and waste time, we want to get there some-time this year, right? Shit, I'm not a mind reader, any-way."

"Mind reader? Couldn't you tell..."

"Ohmigod, must we get into this? It felt like you came, I don't know."

"*Bitch*."

"Wanna keep those eyes on the road, *Dear Heart*?"

Fifteen minutes later, Maryland road stop

Didn't think the blood would freak him so much. Oh well. He's in the bathroom right now, washing it all off. And it felt so good before. All coating his penis like red glazed sugar on a candy apple. Thought he'd be into it. In the ladies room again. The subtle scent of cedar adds a rustic touch, here. Look up and notice the black starry sky from the slated roof. It's all open up there. I check and see that the ceiling over the toilets is intact. Why isn't the area over the sink? Guess it's okay if someone wanted to peek at the chicks washing. Go in stall and notice the uninspired graffiti. *Ann loves Greg 9/5/86-??*

Janine New Jersey on the way to Disney 6/87. Womon to womon we smell and taste better and we know how to pleasure each other. Vic-O-Danny (a circle because hearts are meant to be broken). I become especially ill after reading that one. Retch. I take my handy dandy box cutter out of my bag and dike my finger. Use the blood for ink. *Billy fucked Lisha 7/7/88 (because cherries are meant to be broken).* Yummmm. Too sweet. Impulsively add in ink now, *Lindenhurst, L.I, on our way from hell to here.* Back to the concession stand. Billy, of course. Glom a huge bag o' jujubes from the newsstand on the way. Can tell by the way he glares at me that he still hasn't gotten over his dick. I bop over, hook my finger in his belt loop, say *sorry* so sweetly and kiss his peachy cheek. He pulls back. Turns away. I know how to play *that* game. He's thinking of how to get me back. Tell him *fine* and stomp away. He is smart enough to follow. Happy, but keep my face Valium calm.

I-95, somewhere near DC:

"Hey Billy, what's your Mom gonna say, do you think? I mean, she's actually cool, you probably could have told her that we were blowing. I mean, she might have said it was okay."

"Nah. S'okay. She'd understand it had to be done this way."

"If I told mine she'd try to send me to confession and mass every fucking morning, no doubt."

"Why, does she think the highway is sacrilegious or something? Didn't you come down I-95 once before with her?"

"Don't remind me."

Rest stop in Virginia

A real fancy sort of place. Decadent, even. Sbarros!
Want to call Jenny. See how she's dealing with the
fanatic. Like has our Nunny carved the stigmata into
her palms again last Friday so she'd be most popular
parishioner. Phones upstairs. I get there and see all
kinds of people, especially Suits. Strange, this time of
night. Even find a cute one to talk to. Young. Blonde
hair, Valiant cut. Navy pinstripe, not my thing, but
Billy doesn't necessarily know this. Bop on over to the
guy. Play up my girly thing. He looks at me. I smile in
that way. Take his hand, lead him away, from his
phone call. He has no choice. Likes it even? Massage
his palms with my fingers. Lead him over to Billy, this
way, all teasing, but still no words. Billy seethes. In for
it. He and Suit, eye to eye. Billy, gorgeous scruff, juxtaposed with pin striped yuppie makes me want to juice.
Yuppie is confused. Has erroneously thought me the
innocent. Hell, I can *play* the innocent just fine. They
all like that, initially, until it comes time for real business. Billy, tatters and metal pieces versus cute yuppie
scum. Yuppie bails. No matter. *Fait accompli.* But, forgot to call Jenny.

I-95, near Richmond, VA, after two hours of silence:

"Speak, my sullen one. I'm bored. Or else I'll go to sleep
and then what'll you do, *Lovey*?"

"Fine, Lish, I'll speak.

"Thought so."

"What was up with that shit in there?"

"Huh? Oh, the *Suit*, you mean. Thought he was

cute. Mmm, also to teach you a lesson, of course. Anyway, you know it's you I love."

"Like, what the fuck?"

"Like, I think you know, *Dear Heart*."

"*Bitch*."

"Now you're talking. I could just suck your dick now, you know, but I'm tired. I guess I'll conk out. Have fun driving in this wasteland, *Baby*."

Several hours later, North Carolina Welcome Center

Wake up and realize the car is so hot even though it's night, or perhaps early morning. Pitch dark except for the parking lot lights. Could cook on the vinyl seats. Billy asleep in the back seat. Maybe let this one slide. That was pretty low of me before. Maybe give him a little preview of what's to come. Have to wake him up. Climb over the seat and straddle his skinny body. Grind my jane in his dick. He barely stirs. Slower. It gets hard. His eyes open up and I am his dream. Lids heavy, eyes teary, blurry. Horny though, that's for sure. But won't do him until he makes the trip. That's the deal. Keeps him going, on the move, under my spell. Whip out the blade. Carve myself first, on the spot of my lower belly where the shirt doesn't meet the jeans. Smear the beauty. Looks *too* good that way. The sun is rising now, and he's so turned on, he starts begging for it. Unzip his pants. Grapes. I lick my arm, warm viscous red on my lips, teeth and tongue. Lean down and kiss his dick three times, (three is the charm), leaving bloody lip imprints. He comes right as I sit up. He never takes too long. That was fun. He grabs my waist and smears his white t-shirt with the blood on my stomach. We both die laughing and roll out of the car.

Mouseketeers' mouths in dismay all around us in the early morning heat. Hand in hand, we stroll inside to get pamphlets and do some shocking. Have that warm feeling in my stomach. Full of glee. I know why I did all of this. I know why I took this trip. Ran away from Long Island Hell. We're gonna make it all over this country. But Disneyworld first. Love Billy. Gotta pee. Bathroom is clean and smells of green lollipops.

I-95, fifty miles north of South Carolina:

"There's another one. *Pedro is waiting for you gringos. Rooms from twenty five bucks. South of the Border, fifty miles.* I love these tacky signs. Pure highway trash. Twenty-five bucks wouldn't put us too much in the hole, Lish. What say?"

"Hmm. But can you actually survive sleeping with me cuddled around you naked and stuff with no nooky?"

"Fuck it. We'll keep driving. Only about ten hours or so after S.O.B."

"You got it. Oh cool, they've got, like, fireworks. That sign said, *Pedro's firework factory.* Let's check it out, okay? I love fireworks. Hell, it's as good a place as any to stop for awhile and stretch out at least."

"That and eat."

"That and give these hicks and tourists an eyeful, no doubt, *Babycakes.* I need to get stoned. Pedro's gotta have a headshop."

"At a fucking tourist trap for folks on their way to Disney with their sweet little angels? Get real, Lish."

"I'm as real as the blood oozing from your lip, *Dear Heart.* I was there once, remember?"

"Yeah, with your Mom, the nun. I'm sure you didn't

see more than some stuffed animals and shit."

"Look, Mom the *ex*-nun brought little Lisha and Jenny, and we were looking for fun, okay? I wasn't much different when I was eight. I was into whatever my mom was trying to keep me away from. You can call it precocious, *Dear Heart*."

"Whatever. There's just no arguing with you, Lisha."

"From what I can remember as a little kid, they sold all kinds of sex gags. My mom would try and steer me over to the back-scratchers and Jesus paraphernalia, but I knew. That place is equivalent to an *über* rest stop, *Honey*. The mall of rest stops, okay? Yippee. Hey, pop in that new Ministry album. I wanna sing!"

South Of The Border, South Carolina

Fireworks and sex gags. It don't get any better than this. Huge sombrero'd tower one hundred feet above the parking lot. Fake terra-cotta motels, souvenir shops, restaurants. Stucco. Depression. Ugly Tex-Mex decor. Makes Lindenhurst look like Great Neck. We go into a store together. Wander apart. Piñatas of Jesus, without loot, no doubt. Hats jeweled with mirrors. T-shirts with trite sentiments. The stereotypical middle-aged white trash woman with huge striped shoulder bag pawing through the marked down jelly sandals for her daughter. Look for Billy. He's by the counter. Go over to see what is fascinating him. Tiny greeting cards. At closer glance, notice naked people on the front looking as fatuous as drunken donkeys. Naked. Open the card and a huge dick in pop-up art. *Sheath your sheath, No glove no love*, other such puerile phrases. Glad, because I think of the children who can benefit from this. Must be their demographic. Or dumb-fuck hicks. But children matter more to me. *Blessed be the children.* So I spy a child. Flaxen locks, red heart-shaped sunglasses, pink shorts outfit. Around six. Giggling at the Pedro doll that talks Spanglish when you pull the string. I want to educate her. Prevent her from getting AIDS. Show her the card. She giggles at the big dick. Before I can stop her, runs over to polyester Mom, who's still fingering the jellies, to show and tell. Mom flips, asks where she got such filth. Typical mother. Count on this girl getting pregnant or diseased by the time she is fifteen. Well, I tried. Motor before polyester Mom can find me. Grab Billy by the collar. Leave. Onto bigger and better. The fireworks store. I look around, wistfully I'm sure, for I can't afford to waste money on such delicacies. I finger the lady fingers. Eye the cherry bombs; I can taste their sweetness. I wanna masturbate with one of those Roman Candles. I stroke one and Billy grabs my hand...don't even fantasize about it, he warns me. We can't afford it. *Let's go eat,* I moan. Cherries? Lets blow S.O.B., I'm too depressed to even eat here. We melt into the car seats, then Billy burns rubber. My official assessment of S.O.B.: say it easy; say it cheesy, leave it sleazy. But it don't mean a thing.

Shoney's, South Carolina:

"What is this shit, biscuits with sausage gravy? Fucking disgusting!"

"Lisha, chill out. It's a Southern thing."

"Oh, like sex with siblings and animals is a *Southern thing*, I guess...okay, I'll try not to regurg my cherries, though that would probably taste better than 99 percent of the shit on the menu."

"*Shit*—it's food, Lish. Food I plan on eating, see I'm starved, so shut the fuck up."

"Will you just *look* at those porcine crackers decked out in festively colored polyester gathering around the breakfast bar? It's full of donuts, cake and danish. How healthy. No wonder...oh wait there's also some hash browns, pancakes and bacon."

"Look, are you hungry or not?"

"Yeah. I just want a bagel and O.J. This place is boring, besides."

"*Bagel?* Lisha, this is the deep South."

"Look, that's not the only thing. I'm bored. You can only look at polyester toothless wonders for so long."

"What the hell did you expect?"

"Just some sanity. Mmmm, I miss the city, I guess. You know this is a racist establishment. 'Shoney' used to be a derogatory term white Southerners would call black people."

"Hi, y'all, can I help you kids?"

"Hi, tell me, what do *y'all* have that never breathed or was created, conceived or concocted by vigorous artificial processes?"

"Give y'all a few minutes?"

"No, wait. *Ma'am*, come back here. I just saw that woman who refills the troughs in the *breakfast* bar scratch her twat, madam. That's some sort of health code violation, I am sure. Also, do you prefer to hire only white people or something? This place is pathetic."

"Can I help you, ma'am?"

"Where the hell is your manager, *sugar?*"

"Lisha, just calm down. I didn't even see anything."

"*Hello?* Who asked for your opinion, *sweetie?* I NEED A MANAGER OVER HERE PRONTO! HELLO? I NEED A MANAGER OR I'M GOING TO BLOW THE LID OFF THIS OPERATION. I KNOW MY RIGHTS AS A CONSUMER!"

"Miss, miss, *please* keep your voice down. I assure you, we here at Shoney's only want to please our valued customers. What seems to be the problem?"

"Well, *sir*, I absolutely refuse to eat in an establishment which permits its employees to publicly display self-stimulatory behavior and then, to top it off, touch and probably contaminate the food with crabs or something, from the looks of her. Or is fingering yourself in front of your *valued customers* a form of entertainment?"

"Yes, ma'am, what can I do for you? I'm sorry for your unpleasant experience here at Shoney's where we only want to please our valued customers."

"Well, I am extremely disturbed. I don't even know if I can ever eat here again. Well, maybe you can do *something* to eradicate the situation."

"Ma'am, breakfast is on the house. Anything you like."

"You think breakfast is what I'm after? Can you be so simpleminded?"

"Thank you for visiting Shoney's."

I-95, near Savannah, Georgia

Don't know why I agreed to drive for a while. I guess because Billy looked like he was about to crash any minute. He wanted to stop for a nap, but no way, I said. Felt like driving anyway. Just want to get *there*, now.

So, I'm driving. Big deal. Southern heat so intense the road is pitch black up ahead, then when you get close, it shimmers up and the black evaporates and the road is gray again. Boring people in all the cars that surround me. I despise sameness. All overloaded with blankets and giant bags of no-frills potato chips blocking the windows. Station wagons full of snotty children waving, then giving the finger. I slow down to 60, and teach these two a new one. Tongue wiggling between the V of my fingers. They giggle and try to show Mommy and Daddy. I speed up ahead and notice as I'm passing them, Daddy is getting a hand job. Think it's wonderful they can express their love in front of the children that way. Healthy warm attitudes. Honk my horn and wave. I notice his cum is blood. My head is burning. Speed. Southern downpour thunders on us and it's like we're existing in a car in a cloud. The cloud is so comfy. But then *she* enters the cloud. And now I'm bleeding...my mother into different colors, cutting with glass. Lots of little pieces of glass. Her palms are leaking for real this time. Mere seconds later she's not of flesh any longer, but a window made of stained glass. Stained by the colors of her blood, and other fluids. Grape soda that I had from lunch, maybe. Dirt and ugly flowers from the roadside are added as well. Now she's perfect. She's spitting mud, blood and glass. Yep, this is how I like her. She doesn't even attempt to inhibit me this way. Well, except for my driving, that is, as the Nunny window takes up the entire windshield. She is completely in front of me and I can't get rid of her by using the wipers. Damn, I want to get rid of her now more than ever. I was too glad too soon. It's hard to see; stained glass has the tendency to hamper visibility, so I look and navigate out of the driver and passenger windows, which are safe from stained glass distortion. Check the AAA road map, and realize I turned off on a wrong road earlier. Have to get back on I-95 South. *Speed up.* Look for an exit. The trees that surround the road are tall and they look like they'll eventually strangle the road, since they barely allow two lanes of highway as it is. So *happy.* Maniacally so. Just won't look out the Nunny windshield. Just need to find the turn off point for I-95. But blood is staining the other windows now. It's the trees. Realize I'd better slow down and save them so they are free to strangle the highway. Or maybe then the highway will loop and become a noose to hang myself with. Billy? He's no longer asleep in the back seat. He's outside and bleeding the trees. Need to get him. *Slow down. Slow down.* Slash out at him with a saber and now his blood mingles with the trees, but it doesn't matter, cuz I love him so. He looks all the better for it. The trees are wailing as they are bleeding. There's not a damn thing I can do and notice a cop car appearing, like out of nowhere, at my left. *Pull over, Miss, he says. Mister, it's my boyfriend. No, don't worry about that hag on my windshield. She got hers. It's pay back time for when she tried to pull that one on me. Are you going to do something? I think he is bleeding real badly now. I want to save his ass. He needs a hospital or something. I had to hurt him to save those trees. We must take care of him now. He didn't know what he was doing, officer. But leave that woman on the windshield alone. She's fine that way. As ethereal as she's ever going to get.*

Maggot Motels and Succubi

I'M TAKING A TRIP TO SEE XAVIER in Glen Cove, twenty minutes away. I'm with my best friend, Devon. On the bus we pass this funky old cemetery, and I recall when Billy and I went last Halloween. Billy is my ex. Xavier is my now.

I eyeball Devon and sing, "Hey girlfriend, ever fuck over a skeleton or two?"

She's clueless, of course.

"Uh, yeah, all the time." Her eyes resemble vacant motels. Of course, that's what she thinks I mean. "Bed springs?"

"Duh! Bodies, woman. Maggot motels. Fucking over corpses. Not literally, of course. Separated by six feet, but oh, what a thrill. Remember what that spirit said on the Ouija a few weeks ago? It remembered me."

"You mean the one that said, 'Lisha do blow?' Like, I thought it knew about some time you did drugs or something..."

"Try *blow job*. In a cemetery. Like, on someone's grave, stupid. Oh, man, fuckin' shut the fuck up. Forget the whole thing ever started."

Devon can be so brainless at times. She's too out of it to even be shocked a little. No fun.

Next bus stop and this woman comes on smelling like a mixture of some flowery shit perfume and liverwurst. It hits me that a lot of older women try to cover up a liverwurst smell with tacky perfume. Is it their breath that smells like liverwurst? Whatever, it makes me want to spit on them. Luckily, I have a bottle of pink lemonade that I take a swig from to work up a loogie.

My idea is masturbating my brain. Of course, somehow I attract her to take the seat directly behind Devon and I.

"Fucking *ow*," Devon wails all of a sudden.

The woman must be deaf because she doesn't realize the zipper on her huge Gucci bag, or whatever, has caught Devon's long *Seafoam Green* lock until I reach over the seat and whack her one.

"Excuse me, miss. How dare you?"

And man, is she shooting me one.

I pinch a cut on my arm to infuse my "sweet" psyche with that precious anger. I just glare right back at her. Then I smile, that usually works well. I say nothing.

"Are you going to behave like a young *lady*, or will I have to report this to the bus driver? Because I won't move my seat."

I perceive an imminent diatribe, so I just stare dully at the bitch and quickly choose a response strategy. This tactic has always served to really piss people off.

"I just can't fathom how young ladies of today…"

"Huh…"

"I mean the young women in today's…"

"Yeah…"

"…society are a…"

"Wuh…"

"Disgrace to their sex…"

"Yeh…"

"They don't conduct…"

"Wuhhhh"

"…themselves in a ladylike…"

"Yeh..." I casually give her the finger.

"...*manner*. How *dare* you..." And she's fully incensed and takes another seat, shaking her head, still reeking of liverwurst. *Fait accompli*. And she takes the smell with her.

Of course Devon is *pissing*.

"You fuckin' *rule* girlfriend.

"And don't you forget it." I pat my platinum and *Rose Red* bob, satisfied, too.

We're almost there. I brought Devon with me because she needs a boyfriend, or at least a fuck for Christ's sake. She's always up my ass, so I told X to tell his mildly schizophrenic housemate, Nick, to hang with us. There's something alluring about schizophrenia. It's mysterious, terrifying, and *sexy!!!* If Devon and he were to hook up it would be somewhat hilarious, sort of like a gang bang of the mind, what with all the voices in Nick's head joining in. Of course I haven't told her that he hears voices or that he counts his succubi as women he's fucked. She's psyched to meet him because she knows he is the drummer for X's band, an industrial band that she pretends to know of but probably doesn't. They're called Sybil Sucks One of the Faces of Eve, after the girl bass player who has an alleged affliction of Multiple Personality Disorder. I personally think it's an act cuz she's jealous of all the attention Nick gets for being a Schizo. It's not like this chick is even on Lithium or anything.

"Is he cute?"

Devon likes skater boys. Nick is that, but also a cross between a lobotomized John Cusack and an adorable little spider monkey.

"Sooo fucking hot. You'll *die*."

"Oooh," and Devon giggles.

Can I just mention I hate that? Giggling girls. Gag. I lean over and lick her lips. I know that's sure to piss her off. When I lean back in my seat, I notice my red lipstick mixes nicely with her soot-colored lips. I make a mental note to try that combination sometime.

"What are you doing, Lish? What's with the dyke shit," she asks nervously. I sneer.

"Dyke nothing." I open my journal to signal that I don't want to hear another fucking word out of her black painted mouth.

"This is Glen Cove," I hear the bus driver drone like he's been watching *Dynasty* for too long. Poor guy. When Devon and I pass him by, I stop and run my finger down his arm and smile to make his day. Nothing like an innocent teen girl.

"SSSSSSSSSStttttt." I hear a skank in one of the seats up front. So he thinks I'm a pussy! I'm infuriated that he is even letting my pussy enter his otherwise vacant mind.

Before he can make another animal sound, I leap down the isle, grab his thigh and say really low, "CLUCK CLUCK CLUCK," and he is so off guard by this, and I shout, "Yeah. Like a *cock*, you *motherfucker!!* How dare you dis my Jane?"

He grins like he's such a big man, so I grab his cheap jewels like you'd grab fruit to see if it's rotten and he fucking *freaks*, and then I grin and say, "Be glad you got that for free, baaaabe, your fruit is rancid," and sail out of the bus after Devon. It all happens so fast no one else even knows what transpired. Except my protégé, of course.

"You *rule*, Lisha. I've always wanted to do that to one of those fucking losers."

"Action is what it's all about, girlfriend. You have to be the one to act next time. There is no place to be passive in today's society. You have to show men their place. We have all the power in our hands. They just think they do. Come on, two blocks down, and then Xavier's house is on the right side of the street." I look down at the soft, crumpled paper in my hand.

"3544 Hane Lane."

All of a sudden, Devon grabs my arm, like we're about to sky dive out of some dying DC-10 or something.

"Ah, *hello?!* Do I look like I needed that?"

"Lisha, this is so fucking cool, I can't stand it! Like these guys are in a *band*, man. And they don't even go to our school, so it'll be a mystery to the other kids and stuff."

I roll my eyes. She can be so *high school* sometimes.

We walk up to the tiny bungalow. Xavier's poor. Well, he's a starving musician and I wouldn't have it any other way. Poor is *legit*, see. Not only do Nick and Xavier not go to our school, they don't go to school, period. They're way out of high school. Xavier is almost twenty. Nick just turned nineteen. They live together in this house with Blud, the poser chick with multiple personalities.

I pull Devon over to the hedges next door.

"Time for vanity. Hand me your mirror," I say. She gives it over. I make a horse face at Devon and then at the mirror. Skank mouth check. No food or anything else oozing out from between my teeth.

"Smell my breath," and I breathe on her nose before she can think of having a choice.

"Weed woman," she giggles. "How much did you smoke before?"

"Shit. Just that bowl we shared. Do guys get grossed out by it? Oh, like I care. Do I look okay?" I know I'm stellar, but I have to maintain that certain degree of adolescent girl insecurity sometimes, or no one will like me.

"You always look *awesome*, Lisha. That pink and black vinyl skirt is to die for. Like, when can I borrow it? I've asked you a *mill*."

"In time, woman. Here, take a look," and I hand her back the mirror. She does the once over and I belaud her in reciprocation.

"Seafoam Green is *so* your color. It just totally suits your skin. Brings out your eyes and nails, too."

Devon's hair is really long, so the green makes it even more attention grabbing. Mine's in a bob, which is easier to deal with. She'll get over the long hair thing someday. A throwback to being twelve.

"Thanks." And she giggles. I toss her a threatening glance, so she cuts it.

"Let's blow this pop stand," I say and we're out of the Lawn Doctor's beauty parlor.

"What up," Xavier says when he opens the door. He looks gorgeously bored. I push him out of the way with both hands against his chest and trample into the living room like I own the place. I pull Devon along behind me. I love the aura in the room, which reeks of incense. And Skinny Puppy is blasting out of the stereo.

"'Smothered Hope,' killer song," I comment and flop

down on the infested sofa. Whenever you flop on the thing, something usually alive and usually feeding on something dead flies out of it. The phone rings and I answer it before anyone else can.

"HEllooo," I answer in Blud's affected *come hither* voice. I love doing that—answering the phone in someone else's voice so that the person on the other line thinks it's them. I knew it was for that phone hag.

"Yo, Blud, how's it going?" It is a guy.

"Ohhh, honey, I need it so bad. Why don't you come over nowwwww?"

"Blud? It's Chris, what's wrong with you?"

"Chris?" I look at Xavier and he mouths, "Her brother."

"Oh, sorry Chris. It doesn't matter. I'm sooo horny. I've always had fantasies about you anyway. Come over and..."

"Look, just who the fuck is this?" He sounds pissed. Like I care. I am even getting bored by now, so I shout, "Your Mother!" and I hang up the phone. Xavier collapses on top of me, cracking up.

"You know she's gonna kill you, Lish. I can't understand why you two hate each other so fucking much. Women."

"Oh, don't finish with such a banality. I hate that. She's a cunt, *that's* why I hate her. A lying cunt. Multiple personalities, my ass. She wishes. And the name Blud, how fucking obvious can you get? Hey, she can always say it was one of her other selves who spoke. Devon! Sit the fuck down, you're making me nervous, looming around like that." Now I am sorely in need of something to break. Nick interrupts my moment of angst.

"Hey, you know, if you introduce me to your friend here, I may just share some of that good stuff I got from Terry's brother the other day…"

"Oh Nick, I thought we'd fuck the formalities, I mean, she's standing right there, but since you put it that way, this is my girl, Devon. Now go hit it off and be done with it."

Devon gives scrawny Nick the once over and I know she likes him. When the mental case notices her devouring him, he hastily goes over to the broken down cabinet to retrieve his stash. Devon looks at me and giggles, licking her lips. We all gather on the shabby rug in the middle of the tiny living room, waiting for the primo weed. I have to smoke it sometimes, like when I start to feel ultraviolent. It mellows me out. Otherwise who knows what I might be capable of.

"Hey Nick, don't drugs fuck up your problem? Like I heard that hallucinogens bring out latent schizo tendencies," I sing.

"Nah, that's just the real stuff. Like acid or chemical kinds of stuff. This shit is natural. I can even smoke it when I take my medication," he says as he plops down next to Devon. She's so into him. She digs hearing that he takes medication. Thank God. I have no time for clingers. They always do better elsewhere.

The four of us are sitting—passing the peace pipe, seeing spirits. Surreal hieroglyphics on the living room walls spell out the names of those who died here, and I don't want to be one of them just yet, more like years from now when I'm dried and old, but never complacent. Now sitting, sucking blue out of sawdust, fairy dust, lying back and staring at the brown water stains on the ceiling and I wonder if it will soon cave in because the stains look like oysters on the half shell, all rippled and swollen and if it were to cave in, would someone be sitting in the living room and what would he be doing? Playing music, reading, watching TV, jerking off while fantasizing about that spirit who comes to fuck him in the middle of the lonely night, with those lips sucking him, sucking smoke and he's in a haze. I look at him across from me and think of losing my mind, losing it all, just believing in everything, every image you see, or everything these voices tell you because they are there, only no one else can see them. I stare at him staring at Devon who stares back at him. No one has said a word. The music has gotten louder and no one bothers to speak, only suck more blue and stare back at the ceiling, at each other from time to time and I wonder what is time and how much of it has passed. Nick's foot touches mine and I glance at him, see his hands trace the licorice veins on Devon's arm and she is so gone that she likes it. She is usually as frigid as a Norwegian mountain. He likes her arm, white and blue. Xavier sees me looking at them and pulls at my waist to get me to lean on him. He is a cloud to me and I want to disappear in him. Dissipating like smoke into each other, forming clouds, and X's face appears out of the cloud and is at my face, sucks my lips in between drags of the blue. The water stains are the aphrodisiac in my mind. I arch my back, chest to the ceiling and X puts his hand behind my back and we're in the same cloud. It's raining. I'm sort of aware of the sounds at the window. The thunder, a new voice to Nick, telling him to take off Devon's top. The thunder is God going through his head. Must be. Must be.

Devon giggling, still sucking the blue from time to time. The walls never stop with their storytelling, I wish they were audible too. I am on the outside of the window. Disembodied, just the way I like it, sweet and inno-cent...skin free. I see two girls arched like pelican necks about to break. Devon doesn't look at the wall. She never even really sees the ceiling. I want to remind everyone that Devon has never been in a cloud before. Go easy on my girl. She's soft, unlike me, so hard already. She can't see the sky, the clouds for what they really are. I'm back in and engulfed in the cloud with X and I can't see out. Blue can be better than magic for me.

"What was that, Nick?" Devon is all dreamy-sound-ing. Naked. The blue still surrounds us, but is some-what cleared. Perhaps hours have passed. I don't care. Light blue does me fine.

Nick traces her arms and shoulders, and says softly, "I said, 'I think you've made Lilith jealous. See her standing over there, glaring at us? Hey Lilith, see, I don't need you after all, so I guess you're not so smug anymore. Devon is twice the woman you are and she has real *flesh* besides. Go on, get off my turf. I've found a new love now. And she doesn't make me beg for it or stare at me with scorn."

(*Real flesh, real skin??*) I look over at the two of them entwined like barbed wire, and Nick looks satis-fied with his show of bravado. *I am the fucking KING of my mind, man. I fucking RULE.*

I check the room. No sign of a Lilith anywhere. I wonder how Devon is taking Nick's lack of reality. She's giggling at him. I think he has charmed her with his psy-chosis. X is envious and horny, so he tugs me into his room.

"I think they hit it off. I'll pat myself on the back now," I say, still disconnected.

"Ooh, baby, I'll pat you instead."

"Ooh. Ah. You turn me on with your words, X," I say in a bored, flat voice. "More, I wanna hear *more*." The look in his eyes indicates that he thinks I'm into him. Into it. Ha! His eyes are all loopy. He is a hound.

"Look, I really just want to slam the shit out of you right now," I murmur. "Do you got any Sade?" I'm feeling back in touch with myself.

"No, baby, but I got *this*."

Ugh. I might have to kill him for that. Or at least break up with him. Billy always liked when I got violent. We'd get violent together. That's love, man. Being able to trust someone enough to throw you around and bang you up and shit but not kill you, and then, letting you do the same to them. A fifty-fifty situation. This mushy, lovey-dovey bullshit is enough to make me retch. I thought that since X looks so fucked up, with his mangy digs, he'd be cool. I was way off. Pure sap. But I'll give him another chance.

"Hey. Get me some of that incense."

"Now?" he asks disappointedly. "Why now?"

"Oh, it's for some fun in bed. *Baby*," I add as an afterthought. I hate using or hearing that fucking word or anything like it, unless it's meant to be ironic. Billy used to say that to me too. But mentioning baby and bed in the same breath gets him up off the bed, to get what I want.

"What're you gonna do with it?" he asks excitedly. I light it, let the flame meet the end, let it burn, and blow on it until it glows red. Then I slowly bring it to the baby-soft part of my inner arm and hold it there for a moment and the sweet perfumed patchouli mixes with a more pungent scent of singed flesh. Before I can let it sink in for a bit, like my skin is candle wax, X grabs my hand.

"Come on Lisha, don't do this shit to me now. Damn, girl. You just had to kill the mood. *Fuck.*"

I kiss him on the lips real long.

"I can do it to you? Or you can do it to yourself. As long as I can watch, of course."

"What, you mean like jerk off or something? Hell yeah, I'd be into—"

"No! Burn itty bitty holes into your arms. Or elsewhere if that's more exciting. I'm open-minded."

"Listen, girl, you're like real *whacked*, okay? I mean, I just wanna get it on and you gotta lay this bullshit on me. If you're not interested, just say so. Jesus."

I am bored. Xavier bores me in bed. The music bores me. The faces around me bore me. Hell, at this point the wallpaper even bores me. Sometimes I get this way after I smoke. I just want to be away from the human race. I want to go home.

I go back into the living room, where Nick and Devon can't find it in themselves to locate a fucking *room*, for Christ's sake. They are entwined naked forms on the carpet caked with ashes. Devon is giggling. Nick is talking to another nonexistent person. I stand directly over them.

"Devon, let's get the hell out of here."

"Oh, come on Lisha, I'm having a blast here."

I lean over her, lick my finger and trail muddy designs into the ashes on her skin. She's no longer mine, though. I glare into her eyes and grab her up from the floor.

"Tell me you're still into this. I am bored with it by now and I haven't even spent the past hour *fucking* him." As an afterthought I say, "I may as well have been though. HEY NICK! How many girls *do* you think you were fucking?"

Devon giggles. Giggles again.

"I dunno, Lish. You were there," Nick drawls.

"Oh, so I was there? I'm going to have to discuss this situation with you, Nicky." I sit on his chest. I talk to him sweetly, like he's a little boy. "You see, you violated me, *Baby*. Who knows what may have happened during this alleged fuckfest. You might have offered me bodily harm without my being aware of it. If I *were* aware of it, who knows, I may have liked it. But you'll never know, will you? A metaphysical orgy is fine if you obtain consent first. This, however, is metaphysical rape. Now that's not fair, is it, Nicky?" I twirl a lock of his bleach blond hair.

"Lisha, chill, babe, you liked it, trust me."

He thinks I'm playing with him. Good.

"Like I'll take your word for it. No. It's a control thing. According to you, my little *psychobaby*, I fucked you. According to me, I didn't. But it's not worth arguing. Since I can't alter your perceptions, let's try something. I *know!* I can tinker a bit with your brain so you forget about your temporary delusion."

And before he can say another word, still smiling and sweet, I crush his face with my combat boot. Always knew they'd come in handy. I crush it like it was a slimy slug, spreading the wealth on the bottom of my shoe. But I am yanked without warning, before I have the satisfaction of knowing his brain has swished around in the swampy liquid in his skull. Before I can make any advances in medical science. Xavier.

"Whoa, hold up, girl."

"Now you've really *really* made me *pissed*, X. First you put me to sleep in bed and now you prevent me from helping your *bud* here to see things as they are. You're not even worth exchanging harm with."

Nick is crying. Waaaah. How it breaks my heart to see a lunatic cry. Devon is pissed.

"Whas the matter, you too frigid for an orgy?"

I go over to her and ravage her. Totally tongue her throat until she's crying too. My work is done.

"Homophobe! You think you're so cool, just 'cause you fucked a potential asylumite? No thanks. Look, I'm blowing this joint. Are you coming with or are you going to stay here with Looney Tunes?"

"I'm not leaving yet. I'll get home somehow."

"*Whatever*, Devon."

How do I know that tomorrow everyone in the whole fucking school will know that Devon has a new boyfriend who's a musician *and* schizophrenic?

Today wasn't a total loss, though. Maybe I didn't make a breakthrough in the medical field, but Nick will appreciate what I tried to do for him someday. Care in the guise of cruelty.

Skin

"DESIGNS," I SAY, unwilling to back down.

"No. Like, words are much cooler. They make people wonder what it might mean," says Devon.

"And designs don't? They're not as fucking obvious. Mystery, think *mystery*, girlfriend. And just remember, this little brainchild is mine. My idea."

"Fine, but I'm still doing a word. How good can a design come out anyway? Even if you *are* an artist?"

"It *will* come out fine. I just have to perfect it. Hone my craft. Don't you worry," I continue.

"If you say so, Lisha. So we're going for tomorrow afternoon?"

"Tomorrow."

We do our goodbye ritual, licking each fingertip and then touching each other's, five tips against five.

"I just know we're gonna make the other girls *die*, Lisha."

"Yeah, and you know, the day after, half of them will want to be sporting designs. We're going to rule that school."

We crack up. She leaves. Devon and her silly popularity thing. I know how to play her. Devon is a nice kid, but I don't exactly need her for much. She's sort of my experiment; you know, *second in line*. She'll help spread the joy. So, we'll see how it goes. One thing's for sure. Life at Westend School for the Arts—the trends, movements, and mentalities, at least, will never be the same.

I am standing in front of my mirror, staring at how boring I look. Staring at my pure, virgin skin. It desperately needs to be sullied, made raw and different. Thinking of Bandaids in the medicine cabinet. Thinking of that sharp razor blade, the corner of which stabs the heart of my ex-boyfriend, Billy, in a photo on the corkboard to the right of the mirror. He looks striking that way. I take that blade and think that if it is really sharp, and if my skin is as easy as the wood from which I recently carved an Aztec god in sculpture class, then I've discovered yet another form of art. My high school takes pride in cultivating its students' creativity.

So, I take the blade, and make the first cut into my upper left arm. How precious, these tiny gumdrops of blood which appear immediately. I discover, after subsequent work, the blood hardly gets anywhere. It doesn't smear, unless I smudge it right away, which I don't. It doesn't even drip. It clots.

Intent on a design, I don't waste time on getting a tissue, because I don't want to lose my creative flow. Luckily, the skin also peels into curls (much like when you drag your fingernail alongside a candle), and this makes designing a bit neater. Of course, this all has to be done with precision, or else there could be quite a volcanic eruption of skin and blood. I file this musing for later.

I pause, thinking of road maps—bunches of squiggly lines that can so often be overwhelming. I think of my last road trip (if you can call it that) with my ex, done clandestinely of course. My mother never would have gone for *that* brand of wild, hypocrite that she is. We got fucked up because I couldn't follow the damn road map. I get excited when I get lost. A cracker cop stopped me in fucking *Georgia* of all places. I think I must have threatened him with bodily harm, because he hauled us in, called Mom, and that was the end of being in temporary remission from ennui. To be honest, everything happened so fast I can't remember at this point. You know how it is when all things seem to happen at the same time. It might have been last week or last year. It's all surreal to me at this point.

I keep designing. The skin surrounding the cuts is getting puffy, like an indignant reaction. On the down swirl of a circle—this is not as easy as it seems—I dig in a bit too deep, and a large pearl of blood interferes and halts my precision. I blow on it and feel the sting of a paper cut, times ten maybe. Curiously, I wasn't aware of any pain before this. I get a tissue to wipe it off, but it is like Jello and simply won't come off without messing up the cuts. I stick my nail under this pearl, slice it off and set it aside. I finish my work, which ends up looking like some sort of intricate Egyptian design, but more than that. At some angles, it could even look like an impression of a road map. Like any good piece of art, there could be many different interpretations. I dare say even Dali would be proud. I have a print of his melting clocks on my bedroom wall—my nod to the master, along with posters of the Smiths, the Cure and Bauhaus.

Wait, I want more. There's *gotta* be more. I like the stingy feeling. I feel in *control*. Celestially pure.

Yes, I want more. I recall the possibility of a volcano. I know that I could never be as precise with my left hand on my right arm, because I am not yet ambidextrous. So I slash—not as delicately, I admit—the sides of my right wrist and arm, careful to avoid some major vein. No. Killing myself is not what I am going for. I cover all these yummy cuts, which bear a resemblance to curling ribbons, with Bandaids (I have always used a clear, sparkly nail polish to cover Bandaids. It makes cuts and bruises more festive that way, doesn't it?).

Yes, an eruption indeed. The numb feeling tingles my hand and I feel sloppy and out of control, so I stop. I don't like this feeling of pins and needles in my hand, and I sit, waiting for the numb to go away. I knock it against the wall to regain some feeling.

I walk into my first class: 8:50 Honors English. School's a *breeze* for me. There's Devon. She grabs my arm. She doesn't know she has grabbed a rather stinging spot because I am wearing long sleeves. I elbow her in the tit as a reflex.

"Watch what the fuck you're doing, girlfriend." I smile at her. She knows, probably because of the way I yank my arm away, like I'm trying to escape my skin.

"You..." she stutters.

"Yeah," I answer.

"Not showing it all yet?" She's trying to insinuate that I'm scared to show it. Like I'm weak. I throw it back at her.

"I didn't feel like it yet. The designs aren't ready." She'll never win. She's nothing but a follower.

"So, will they be ready tomorrow?" she asks.

"Yeah, man, you have to let it set a day. These things can't be rushed. *Chill.*"

She has no answer for that. I can see the wheels turning in her head. I don't wait for her to keep going on about it. Truthfully, the girl can be quite boring at times.

"Meet me right after school in front of the clock, Devon," I call out casually as I go to the back of the room to sit, as far away from her as possible.

3 p.m. and we meet.

"Lisha, I've been thinking about this all day, and, well, I thought we were in this together. Now you're a whole day ahead of me," she whines.

"Nah. There is no 'together' in this game of pain. Be strong. Be your own person. That's what it's all about."

She looks confused.

"So, can I see yours now?"

I show her. It was raw in the shower this morning. I guess the soap didn't help matters much, it was that Irish variety and green always seems to be the most painful color of all soaps.

The blood work now looks a little more towards a shade of burgundy. It's starting to scab as well. The pretty design is still intact on the left arm. I have been careful all night and day not to tear it by accident. Skin *is* rather delicate. After my shower I had to change to new Bandaids as well. The black gummy rectangles surrounding the sloppy red slashes on the right arm are not all that attractive, unfortunately.

"Nice, but I still want to do a word. I've thought about it. I'll write 'Nick.'" She looks so satisfied with herself. She wants to carve that schizo's name on her body.

"Aww, your boyfriend? Who the hell do you think you are? Sid Vicious? Get with the eighties. I still can't believe you're going out with him after what he *thinks* he does with other girls. Myself included. Ugh."

But she won't budge. *Mediocrity*, I tell you, is something I will always strive to avoid.

We're in my room. I have every bright light turned on. I am even burning candles. The shades are down. I want a feeling of reverence to infiltrate the room. Sunlight ruins things. I take the blade from my ex's heart and make the first cut on Devon's arm.

"See, now it's red and rippled like ribbons. It's *begging* and *crying* to become a design. Are you sure, *absolutely* sure, that you want to carve your schizo boyfriend's name? You might even be broken up by the time the scar is set."

"I'm sure, I'm sure. How long's it gonna take?" Her face is in a twisted grimace. I pity those strangers to pain, those who fear it. Devon's my best friend, and I do care. I have to prepare her.

"You know what? I'm leaving it all up to you now. You know, D.I.Y.? Do it yourself. It's almost a spiritual thing. I'd be ruining it for you if I carved for you. I even need to leave the room, Devon."

"Ohhh. But your handwriting is better than mine," she whines.

God. I really have my work cut out for me. But I must teach her to be self-reliant, even if she can't be a real artist. It's a big part of this.

"Take your time and it will come out alright. It has to be *your* thing."

And I leave.

Today's the day of the "opening." My bandage-free debut. Devon has to wait a day to let the cut settle, same as I did. It's crucial that I go first.

8:50 Honors English. I make my entrance, just as the last bell rings. Last one in the door, and that's no accident. I'm wearing a tank top. Arms sleeveless, bare and beautiful. The well-crafted designs on the top of my left arm. First fierce red, then burgundy, and now regal brown. The haphazard whim on my right arm is still covered with Bandaids.

I hear the kids begin to buzz and the buzzing turns into the girls oohing and aahing and the boys saying things like "wicked."

I see Devon with a jealous look on her face and give her the smile of serenity. All she cares about is popularity. I'm interested in a new school order. And art for art's sake.

I hear a throat being cleared as I reach my seat.

"Lisha, can I speak to you outside?"

I follow Ms. Kramer out of the class.

"So, what's the deal with those slashes on your arm," she begins sardonically.

I look at my right arm where the slashes are. I am confused because they are still covered by the Bandaids. Then I see her staring at my left arm. My *designs?* Slashes? I think not. I talk to her in my *I guess you're retarded voice.*

"You mean these designs, Ms. Kramer? It's for one of my art classes."

"*Art class?* Who is your teacher? What kind of assignment is *that?*"

"It wasn't an *assignment.* I am not ruled by *assignments.* I am an artist. DIY and aberrance. That's what *art* is all about," I explain. I don't expect a mere English teacher to understand.

"Well, this is just...this is just...*beyond* me. Maybe you should go talk to Doctor Owen about this...I mean, it's not very aesthetically pleasing and you could have..."

"Oh, like I give a damn about your aesthetics, *honey.* That's subjective. Just like how you consider drivel like

Anaïs Nin literature, while I'm more of a Poe gal. You dig?"

"Lisha, you're not going to pass off this, this self-mutilation, as art. When you were doing this to yourself, did you consider that you could infect yourself or even worse, cut into a major vein and *die?* Are you suicidal?"

"Ms. Kramer," I begin calmly. "I'm afraid you're projecting some psychological hang up of your own onto me. Perhaps *you* should seek the help of a shrink."

"Lisha, I'm going to have to send you to the principal. I can't allow this so-called creative *butchering* to go unnoticed. Think of the school's reputation. You could be setting a bad example for others, too. I encourage you to tap into your creative reservoir for a new type of art."

"I think you need to get off your fat ass and go look at the school's mission statement that graces our entrance hall. I am merely expressing my creativity. It would be not only grossly unfair of you to discourage me, but also you would also be violating school policy. I don't believe this crap. What's the point of an *Arts High School* if we can't express ourselves as we want? *I will not be censored*. I might even bring you up on discrimination charges. I will go all the way with this, I promise you that."

She is defeated. I see it in her eyes. She tries one more inane tactic.

"And what do your parents say about this," she asks weakly.

Good one.

"My mother knows. *She* encourages all of my creative outlets." Actually, I've avoided my mother the past two days. It's not that hard. She's at church when I leave in the mornings and at her job *du jour* when

I get home in the afternoons. I stay in my room all night. If I have to come in contact with her, I'll just wear sleeves.

She would be more upset about the mess I made anyway. When I really got into the volcano thing, I guess I was hacking and some skin flew all over. A few teeny pieces stuck to the mirror, even. I cleaned it all up yesterday morning. I know that Jenny, who shares my room, won't tell. She worships me. Anyway, she's never around anymore so it's likely she doesn't even know about it.

I continue to stare Kramer in the eye. "Hmm," I say. "I guess you're just too conservative for this sort of self-expression, you quixotic aging hippie. I bet the *younger* teachers will appreciate it."

"Look, Lisha, maybe there's nothing I can do about this right now. But this self-mutilation won't go unnoticed. It's not over."

"You have a class to teach," I remind her. "I'm going in."

I sail into class, winner all the way. All around me, the buzzing, oohing, aahing and words.

"Lisha, cool arms. They're so pretty. Will you do mine?" I hear Ashley, most beautiful girl on campus, say. I have to think her over. She may be just a tad shallow.

"Talk to me after class."

"Pay you ten bucks."

"We'll talk later."

Just three days later and there's this skin frenzy. I have cultivated a small, distinct following of carved teens I've come to fondly refer to as "Designers." (I've transformed four others since Devon) Everyone else looks up to us and probably secretly wants to be carved too. But I am selective. I have to know their motives, for starters. Poseurs are screened the hell out by a brief interviewing process.

First question: "If you had the chance to burn all the record albums of one rock band, which would you choose?"

(This would be almost any Top 40 band, with bonus points for one of the following: Journey, Bon Jovi or Genesis.)

"Who would you kill if you could get away with it?"

(Now, if someone were to say Reagan, well, that's an automatic in.)

"Why do you feel the need to start carving your arms?"

(There is no pat answer. I like to see a variety of answers here. Of course if one lamely answers, "because it's cool," or "because I want to piss my folks off,"I say, "Get the fuck out of my presence. Don't come back until you've done some soul-searching and have a less trivial motive.")

Once allowed "in," I help kids cultivate their ideas, get them started with the first cutting, and then they finish the design themselves. They then become one of us: a Designer.

The whole school has changed, I tell you! There had been a static quality to the air here at Westend and I've cut through it all. Who knows what's next? I see underground ubiquity as the inevitable outcome here. They all tell me how I've changed their lives. I'm amazed how they're just rejecting their weaknesses like a body does its entrails after some severe recreation gone bad. Some first-hand accounts:

"Lisha, after you left the room, and I was cutting, I felt like I was transformed onto another *plane* or something. So I carved an impression of an airplane. Thanks, Lisha."

"Lisha, I feel so in *control* of my body, now. I've even stuck to my diet and lost weight. How can I show my appreciation?" (Usually, I ask for a one time donation of fifteen bucks, for my cause, and materials—not that you can put a price tag on these things.)

Sure, there are those who resist. I say, fine, let them discover their own thing. There are leaders, and then there are those who look for guidance. I do what I can for people. They look up to me now. I overheard one kid telling his friend that I am the unofficial guru of the entire school. All I can say is, pain can sometimes be a therapeutic art. It took someone with foresight to get people's attention. There's not a damn thing anyone can do to stop me either.

Late one afternoon Principal Flaid calls me into his office. I float in and sit directly in front of him. I'm wearing another one of my favorite tank tops.

"Lisha, I see what Ms. Kramer has told me is true. I was inclined to just let this sort of thing slide; we do like to encourage our students in expressing themselves in whatever form they like. I mean, several students have unconventional hair colors; boys with pierced ears even. We have no problem with that. But in your case, Lisha, I just don't believe you realize the implications of your act. By harming yourself in such an irresponsible fashion, you have also served as the impetus for other students to follow suit. The least you could have done was keep this to yourself. Now, I have several hysterical mothers calling me, asking what we are encouraging here. I'm afraid I'm going to have to nip this trend in the bud, or it will get really out of control. Two weeks suspension, starting tomorrow. I am sorry, but we have to set some sort of boundaries here, or what next?"

I just nod at him. There's no point in trying to make him understand. He's trying to cover his ass. Why should I have expected anything else? Of course, I am undaunted. This isn't the end. We'll just operate sub-basement. A sub-basement movement lends itself to the notion of art as a perversity. I am confident that some-day my vision will be realized.

"I see you are taciturn. Am I getting through to you? Art is not supposed to hurt other people. It's sup-posed to enlighten them, make them appreciate things they have never seen before. Things they can't even *fathom*. No, I won't pass judgment. That's not what this meeting is about. This is something for you to think about over the next two weeks."

I am inspired. I have two weeks now to do whatever I want. I smile at him, and he is confused by my reac-tion. He probably expected some rebellious youth. I like to catch them off-guard. Better that way, so he forgets about me and goes on to more important issues, like keeping the number of same-sex teacher affairs a secret.

I'm walking out of Flaid's office and Devon walks up to me with a shit-eating grin.

"I have two words for you, Lisha, *finger digits*."

"Say *what*?"

"The next big thing. Amputating the first digit of the finger and replacing it with a silver or gold one."

"You don't know a damn thing about art, Devon. Stick to your dancing or whatever the hell it is you do in that musty room full of graceful cookie purgers. Leave the next wave to me, *dearie*."

Finger digits. There's no art in prosthetics. What the hell is her problem? I knew she was in it for superficial reasons.

Viking Tales

I AM A BABY-SITTER. That is my job. Not my profession. Just a job. The kiddies, my kiddies, love love *love* me. They gaze at me with wonder in their eyes. I tell them stories unlike the ones my Nunny told me, and I do better: I tell *reality* tales—*Viking Tales* rather than the banal tales of the Fairy—and I give them candy before I begin. Oh, my little kiddies of caramel and cane. My precious darlings. Alan and Nancy. They adore me. They feel safe with me. And so I begin...

Mummy's Little Girl

Once upon a time there was a pretty Wee Girl. Her hair was golden with the texture of a soft cherub's ass. She had baby lips. Lips that sucked, sucked on lollies and sugar metal tits that spurted forth cotton candy. So this Wee Girl with perfect hair loved for her Mummy to fix it in all sorts of styles. And Mummy used a special sort of hairpin to create spectacular styles. The girl was the talk of the second grade. But no one really knew what was going on. Every day the Wee Girl would come downstairs, constellations in her eyes, and call to her Mummy, "I'm ready!" And Mummy came running with the special pins in her hands. They were magical pins. Her Mummy was a fairy.

A small hand grasps my arm. I am tickled and hand out more charms. The kiddies stare transfixed, and I smell chocolate seeping from their mouths.

These pins *appeared* to be bobby pins with safety rubber ends. But that was just an illusion, because Mummy stuck the pins all the way in, into her sweet little head. All the way in like her head was made of cake! It hurt the Wee Girl, but the pins had a special beauty spell. She wanted to be the prettiest girl in the school. And that's just what Mummy told her she was, so she really believed everything was fine, smiled like a Cabbage Patch Kid, and went to school. She thought she had so many friends 'cause her hair was so special, but in reality they kept far, far away from her. Before she went to bed every night, Mummy would give her hot milk with almonds and honey, a forget-me-herb, and the Wee Girl fell asleep, a blissful sweet sleep with her scalp reattaching itself, filling in the teeny tiny holes, and she woke up to a new day and a new hairdo.

I feel the children trying to clutch on to me. I kindly shrug them off.

These herbs must have been extra strong because one day she woke up one hour late. Mummy liked to sleep late and trusted the Wee Girl to be her darling wake-up call. She had exactly 15 minutes to get ready, eat, and go to school. She put on her clothes and walked to school without waking up Mummy. She even forgot about her hair, that's how worried she was. When she walked into her classroom—the last one in—everyone's mouths just dropped open as if she was the boogeyman's daughter, and indeed, she could have looked no worse. And she couldn't believe the looks on the faces of all her "friends."

Chubby hands on ears. I quickly remove them.

She touched her hair and felt a thick wetness. What

was on her hands was like a bloody mess of Kleenex. She ran to the bathroom and looked at the mirror. What was left of her hair was covered in blood and pink skin. It was so thick it didn't even drip. Just like a gelatin snack.

They try to hide from the story. I pull them back beside me.

She then remembered exactly all that Mummy had done to her. Ah! The horror for the Wee Girl. To realize your Mummy is nothing but an evil witch! When the Wee Girl went home, her Mummy ate her after seasoning her with garlic and herbs. That Halloween no less than 8 girls and 14 boys in all of the school, grades one through six, dressed up as this wee girl I am telling you about today.

Weeping. The sweet weeping. I pull out a charm and it does the trick. I wonder how Walt Disney would handle this story. After all, in the Hans Christian Andersen tale, the Little Mermaid really dies. (I always tell the children the real endings, when I run out of my own stories.) It's not fair to fool children. They know they won't be as popular as the wee girl on Halloween, but they can be happy that their heads won't ever be a Play Dough Fuzzy Barber Shop head waiting to happen. They will become suspicious of adults and I cannot emphasize the importance of this enough. This story is good for Nancy. She has been spending an excessive amount of time in front of the mirror lately, trying to emulate her High-Mai mother.

Now, every boy I know hates stories with pretty princesses and fairies, or girls of any type for that matter. So I, not one to show favoritism, try to accommodate these young chaps to the best of my ability. My secret? To employ, then destroy delusions about "heroes" (Alan is presently the star of his little league team). First though, I pass out the Twinkies and Yodels.

The Little Boy Who Couldn't

Once upon a time there was a little boy who was excessively proud of the medal he won for running the fastest out of all the kids ages 8–10 in the tri-state area. He wore this medal everywhere—to bed, even. Every day he would show up to his fourth grade class wearing the colors of his track team—blue and gold. And the medal, of course. Everyone, including his teacher, Mr. Graham, would watch him admiringly as he walked in, always last, so everyone could see him make his grand entrance. Life couldn't be better for this fourth grader—he was the pride of his school, his community and his family alike. One night this panther child went to bed, wearing his medal as usual, but little did he know that his jealous older brother had put a black magical spell on it when he had taken it off before his nightly bath. So he went to sleep and was awakened by something running around his room so fast, it was actually windy. All the boy could see was a white form, with his medal. He heard hysterical laughter, which was even more terrifying. "Catch me if you can, boy," it screeched. "That's the only way you're going to get back your medal. That's the only way you're going to wake up. Otherwise you'll stay like this every night forever! Wheeeeee." The boy jumped up and tore after his medal. And it would fly tantalizingly close to his head and just as he was about to reach it, again it would fly out of his grasp. Now, this boy was fast, and he never seemed to tire when running long distances, but after seven hours of running like a madman around his room, over the bed and desk and bookcases, by the time the sun rose, he fell into his bed dead asleep. When his proud mother came to wake him up the next morning, she couldn't rouse him. In fact, he appeared to be in a coma. The next night, he was awakened by this spirit again, and again, he was fruitless in getting back his medal, and fell into a coma-like sleep. After a week of this, his parents and doctor gave up all hope and let him live out the rest of his "life" in his bed, but oddly enough, because of all the exercise he received at night and the nourishing feeding tube during the day, he did not die, in fact he lived a long life. Forever, practically. And every night was the same vicious circle. The end.

Sure, Alan is confused now. He may not want to sleep for a while, but excessive pride is despicable, even in a boy so young. Now is the best time to learn!

One may ask, "What do the parents of these children say?" Hey, I'm not stupid. I know how parents are about sheltering children from the horrible truths of the world. That's probably what Etan Patz's parents tried to do for him, and he vanished when walking home from school, never to be heard from again. Also, let's see the victims of Albert Fish, Richard Speck, and that Night Stalker character. I bet their parents were like, "Oh sweetie, isn't the world just pretty and grand?" Let's just fuck the grandeur for awhile.

   I like to use this next story as a starter for all new jobs—it serves to break in the new kiddies. It works fine for boys or girls, because the sex of the child in the story is irrelevant and the moral is important for all children: don't listen to your parents! Everything is not okay. The world is full of fucked-up adults who will just as soon corrupt you as they will be kind to you. Hone your own instincts and then follow them!

Safety and Sleep In Houses

Once upon a time there was a little Pink Girl who was as safe as an ugly rose in a garden that has no fear of dying an early death by being picked before its time. She was safe in her room, in her safe house, the safest place for a little Pink Girl to be. Well, one night this little girl was awakened by an extraordinarily loud and jarring noise. Think city bus crashing into a van full of Cerebral Palsy folks—all that metal, wheelchairs and stuff.

The children may lose interest here, though. I must always remember the best way to get a kid enthralled by a story is to keep a child as the main focus at all times.

So, in the van full of handicapped *children*, no one was left alive. The noise woke up little Pink Girl. She was dreaming of the accident and was so happy to wake up in her safe, safe bedroom. So she yawned, smiled and ran out of her room, just like a busy little squirrel, down the stairs where she discovered the real cause of the loud, loud noise. And this was a far worse tragedy, you see. Two big bad men had broken into Pink Girl's safe house, so it wasn't so safe anymore. She crouched like a scaredy squirrel on the stairs and watched the two men do bad things to her mommy. And her mommy, boy did she scream, worse than she did on that roller coaster at Six Flags last summer. They were throwing heavy objects, like the VCR with her Cinderella video in it, at her mommy's head, and the screaming was so horrible that Pink Girl just covered her ears and then remembered those fairies who saved the day for Cinderella and even Pinocchio in the Disney tales. Maybe one could save her mommy, who was lying on her back now as one of the big big ugly men was thrashing her biggest Tonka truck against Mommy's head while the other shoved Barbie up her thing. Pink Girl had too many toys. Mommy was in for it. But no fairy ever came.

A good many lessons are to be learned from this: 1) Mommies don't live forever; 2) Bad things come to children who are greedy and have every toy they ever wanted; 3) Fairies never did and never will save the day because there is no such thing; 4) Pink is the color of the weak, and the most important thing: 5) You are never, ever truly safe. Always be prepared and on your guard. No child I ever baby-sit will be mugged, hurt, or killed. And they will always be prepared for the death of a parent.

One particular story I have in my repertoire really gets the kiddies going, especially if they are recalcitrant. They love to hear about Viking Girl the most. Because she is a good example for them, I never hesitate to honor their request. It has turned many a "sugar and spice and everything nice" girl into the Viking she is now because she wanted to be just like the Viking Girl. What's important here is that this Viking Girl really did and still does exist.

The Viking Girl

Once upon a time there was a Viking Girl. She was strong and never played with dolls, unless it was to dissect them and then use their various limbs for artwork.

The Viking Girl hated school because it was so boring and ceased to provide a challenge for her. None of the kids at school really liked her either. They picked on her for a big ugly crucifix her mommy forced her to wear around her neck, and for her clothes that they deemed "out of fashion."

She chose to deny her Catholic upbringing because of her fanatical mother. It was ironic because sometimes this Viking Girl appreciated her childhood. It helped her to become the Viking she is today.

Mom, oh let's just call her Nunny Pie, as she was originally (that is until her snatch lost its grip on itself), brought up Viking and her little sister to be devout. Everything by the book. Perhaps Nunny thought she'd save face that way, for fucking up.

One fun pastime this little family indulged in together was a seasonal activity. A rite, if you will. A fertility rite. But they couldn't call it that back then. The Pagan implications could ruin Nunny. This rite occurred every Spring when the garden thawed into moist vitamin-packed patches of fertile ground. There in the mud, Nunny, Viking and Sissy weeded, raked, seeded and planted flowers. If only Spring was not so inspirational, because that was when Nunny Pie thought up the stigmata scheme. Unbelievable as it may seem, on Good Friday that year, Nunny Pie stood in front of her congregation and proved herself to be an icon (but actually more of an unctuous fraud), palms thrust forward, suppuration apparent to all of the seething parishioners, in the shape of a slit. Nunny wanted to prove her celestial snatch. The dark red liquid was supposed to be Christ's blood, but it could have been cornstarch and cherry syrup, for all I know. Nunny caused quite the sensation. This balmy spring day prior to the birth of Nunny's stigmata, Viking Girl filled a flour pie crust with fresh, moist mud filling. It looked like a thick chocolate pudding. She offered Sissy a hearty slice which she gladly accepted. She even looked like she was salivating a bit over it (chocolate was always her favorite). Nunny watched on in awe, amazed that a silly child could be so crafty and convincing. It was, after all, mud, and Sissy promptly threw up what she stuffed in her mouth. Nunny didn't even kill Viking Girl for it. She got it in her head that such a skillful trait must run in the family. And then she acted on it: totally went about converting the easy-to-convince masses. Those gullible church folk. And it all worked.

At school, the kids gradually began to admire her. *Viking Girl* they called her, because of the braids, and they thought they were poking fun, but they were actually complimenting her. She dressed in a blue gingham dress (and some subsequent days red organdy) to belie her vicious hairdo and Viking attitude. She wore jail tights and authentic combat boots, a hidden dagger lying against her ankle: a perfect juxtaposition of dainty and deadly. One day in school she told everyone that if they fucked with her, she'd carve their pretty faces into hideous masks. One doltish boy thought she was bluffing and waited for her during recess to lick her face, and when he got close enough, she cut a heart into his face. She got suspended for a month and lived happily ever after. The End.

Sometimes I wonder why it is that girls in stories and fairy tales are always these ethereal, nymphish creatures frolicking in gardens? I suppose the garden setting is so darn tempting! Perverting it is fun fun fun, like bomb pops and the Snow White ride at Disneyworld are fun things. All eaten and experienced in one day, that is. Bomb pops seem sweet, and you're actually consuming a weapon, but no one thinks of it that way. The Adventures of Snow White ride looks innocuous enough, but the witch makes it a terrifying ride to any child. Don't gardens seem like breeding grounds for evil?

The Wake

HOW BIG A BOX FOR HER, NUNNY? Cuz here I stand, just wondering. I do hope you know, cuz this means eternity. Come on, *what style* box for a fifteen-year-old girl? Undecided still? Yeah, I should have known better. Here's some help—Will it have a frilly pastel pillow for her head? Will it be satin lining in dark rose, just like her bedroom walls? Will you put in her viola so she can play it if she wishes? Is the box big enough for the both of them? And what about those pictures to depict her strange "beatnik side," I believe is how you used to put it. What about those pictures you took last year when she gave the finger to the camera in a burst of uncharacteristic hatred for you, you silly fanatical bitch. No, she's pure. Still pure. So pure...my sister, eternally pure. Let's keep her that way.

What will she be wearing? Tell me, because I wanna know. That freshman prom dress? Well, now, you'd save money that way. After all, does it make sense to go all out and search for something designer? What fashion *would* be appropriate for infinity? Perhaps a wedding dress, then? That is the Catholic custom, isn't it? No, we all know Jenny did not die a virgin, and you know that everyone knows and you couldn't be so obviously *phony*, now could you?

Will you let her keep the blue nail polish on? Or will you change the color to an appropriate shade of girly pink? There will be three viewings before the final closing. You could change the color to a different *appropriate* color three more times!

And let's not forget the simple makeup. She's quite young—you may recall, so no need to cover any aged skin. Her cheeks will be smooth for days yet. No crows feet to fill out, lips to puff up. She is perfect, except for the blood and breath.

She's drained of blood. And blood makes beauty.

Will you put in her favorite doll? That Monchichi she and I used to fight over. We were both really too old to be playing with dolls, but we couldn't resist this one. Its thumb could fit into its mouth so it was self-nurturing. That little human-like monkey had no need for a Nunny.

Let's not forget those Donny and Marie dolls you picked up for us at the O'Frankel's garage sale when we were 5 and 7. We didn't care that they were out of date. Marie could fit into 12" Barbie replica outfits and that's all that mattered. No, I want them all. I won't give up any of those to a girl who is going into the ground.

When does this whole thing commence? I ask you, before you escort me out of your office, kind sir. No, I don't mind my mother at all. Tomorrow.

The First Viewing Of Jenny

Not black box,
Nor cedar box,
But satin pillow
covered with hair,
come one, come all, into
my sister's lair. A pearly pink box

perfect for a girl, come in,
give her a whirl, give her a go.
With any doubts of—alive—
give her a blow, pretend
she's the candles on a cake,
here, now *you're sure,*
she isn't a fake. This is death, all right,
pristine box or no. But tell me,
tell me
tell me—
how can she have an utterly sanguine glow?

I sing the song, my own unique brand of nursery rhyme hickory-dickory-dock as I look down at her, my Jenny.

She is wearing a yellow cotton dress with spring-time wildflowers on it. The sleeves are cap and the bodice is empire, with the skirt going past her knees. Very appropriate. And very unlike Jenny. My sister would have preferred a dress from the '40s, no doubt, something in the "swing" style. She always loved coming back from the thrift shop with a new dress to mend and make her own. And Nunny hated that.

I finger what's in my pocket and grasp it. The sharpness juxtaposed against the cotton comforts of my pocket. Sweet blade, how I savor thee. I call upon you to ensure our three full viewings of Jenny. This, because I do not trust any modern embalmer of today. He may have left just a drop, just a jewel, and I must ensure this is not so. I must leave more than a mere mark upon my beloved, so that I can have anything, even if only a drop, of what is vital.

So, I take that blade, lift her sleeve and make a ceremonial first cut on the top of her arm, but only a tiny amount of clear liquid, not a hint of red, seeps out. I realize a design is not only possible but necessary as well, but *where* and *what?* I am the cause of her death, for as the parishioners have been whispering, it was all because of me and I am just "evil." Not a good fucking thing about me. And my "poor" mother. *Chris, do you think she was jealous? Could that be it? You never know with girls so close in age. Jenny was a great kid. And Lisha is quite a handful...*They may whisper, but I can still hear. And they really do not need to whisper, do they? Surely not when their faces are such pathetic open bibles. So they know. But how the fuck could they? How did our family's sorry story make it out to this pathetic neighborhood of Long Islander trasheteers? They all secretly love it and revel in the drama of it all. Next thing I know, I'll be on Oprah or the Phil Donahue show so that the bovine ladies of the crowd can look down upon me. White trash drama, as pure as a can of unopened Hormel Potted Meat Product. As perfect as a breakfast of Scrapple and egg replacers, with sickly sweet strawberries in June. Coated in heavy cream and regurgitated for our children to swallow, so they too can be pure. Pure as my sister's virgin skin. Pure as mine used to be...

No thanks. I am like, so out of here.

But first, my mark. On my *beloved*, no matter what they think.

And I continue the blade's disappointing trail. Blood is beauty, after all, and here there is none. No satisfaction, but then I can always go back to my own if I need it bad. And here I am, jonesing for the blade, horny for that exquisite scratch, and always thinking of myself, selfish brat that I am...But I must get myself together to leave the first of my marks in a few simple words...*Lisha loves Jenny forever*—except the word love isn't written. Rather it is represented by a heart, and a bloodless heart at that, so I am compelled now to leave my own beauty as a stand-in, after seeing how blank it looks without...I take that blade on myself now, and make the cut.

On the Second . . .

Here she is in front of me again. Can I believe this? For sure it is she—but sleeveless. I look around me to find the culprit and see no one. I check the wrist—I'm still there. But whoever removed the sleeve, whoever that is, had to have noticed the engraving. Was it our Nunny? I am not even present in her eyes, today or yesterday. She probably wouldn't bother asking me about it.

Jenny is wearing a green dress with yellow daisies today. Who thought of that? Springtime wild flowers, and now daisies. *Who knew about the garden?* This means someone else besides us had to have known. I only know of one other who was there both times, Jenny and Lisha as little girls. Jenny and Lisha as Teens with Issues. Only one other, who grew up alongside us. The weeded nun. Our *mum*, hardly a flower...

This dress proves how little there is left of Jenny. It's like she is almost evaporating before my very eyes.

Vapor of Jenny before my eyes,
like a sweet mist,
sweet little Jenny without her florid fist...

Still alone, I check the room carefully. The parishioners will not arrive for at least another half hour. One or two of them must be consoling Nunny at home. I have time aplenty to celebrate the Second Viewing of Jenny. I stare at her until my eyes are full of her, nothing but her, there is nothing but her, after her, always her. And yet she is evaporating before my very eyes.

I have to leave another mark. I have to draw a flower somewhere. The furious rose.

So, I take that blade and make yet another disappointing cut. Whoever heard of a clear rose? Lack of any color at all. Yes, there are white roses, yellow roses, pink roses, roses dyed purple and black and blue, but what I crave right now is the one and only red rose, and what I get is a clear cut. A clear cut rose. But that is what I must leave and so I do. It's on her left palm, a perversion of our Nunny's "stigmata." I take her hand in my own, and kiss the palm, leaving my red lipstick as legacy to blood.

On the Third . . .

Today, she is wearing a *bikini?* This looks like the work of our slut, Nunny. What was she thinking? Now this is too *garbage blanc*, even for her! But I cast away all ideas of female exploitation and see the inherent possibilities in the situation.

I want to carve a baby into her now useless womb... the baby *it* could have been, the baby it may have wanted to become. With fantastic precision, I take the sweet blade of nurturance out of my pocket and commence the birth of design...

A stroke, a slash
a series of dash, all merrily depicted
in border of tasteful rash,
and so I clap
one time, two times, three times, four,
slamming my palms together,
fucking with the sore,
singing the spell, almost forgetting
what came first and then it's all over me
in a great burst (like a roman candle
spraying spite, I wield my razor
with all of my might).

It's right back in my head, no matter how hard I try to forget, to pretend it never happened. And so instead I carve *It*. The fist, all it would ever be, all I can imagine. I carve until it is no longer Jenny but that which killed her, all in a neat package on the skin covering her womb. Fucking the myth of the garden, I take her palm and destroy the meaningless "flower" I inscribed yesterday. There are no more flowers. And I feel a stirring come from the design, but I ignore it. It seems to come to life, but I ignore it. The designs, they came to life before, but not like this. So it's fine, it stays as it was, a part of Jenny, it stays. Or does it die?

The Wake Continues . . . ?

I enter the gauche funeral parlor only to find a box free of Jenny; she has now evaporated, just like I suspected she would. The flowers surrounding her box is gone. An empty box. I run out of the room, almost in slo-mo, to find who is responsible. Enraged, I come upon some hapless corpse caretaker. I make my face deliberately scary.

"Ah, hell-O? Where is my sister? Her name is Jenny—"

"Miss, I do not know of a Jenny here today. Perhaps she was taken?"

"My sister is gone! I demand her return. I demand you bring her back here for me—"

"Miss! Where is your mother?"

"I don't have what you call, a *mother*. I have a Nunny and I don't care where she is. I am to be contacted for all of Jenny's concerns. You took her without my approval. I am in charge. It's me, don't you see that? What do you see? You see—"

"What I see is a very grief-stricken little girl who needs her mother. Why don't you go home now?"

"FUCK YOU, little man." And I run out of there. I have to find her. She has escaped from her sweet pink box. Escaped from her pink nail polish and girly dresses. Escaped to find the source of her scars.

I have to find my sister. She is gone. She may be lost, who knows? I have to help her. It's always her. Always my Jenny. Always.

She is lost. And I will find her.

two: Finding

FALL 1988/WINTER 1989

I made things.

And on the Day of the Dead...

SWEET...FUCKING...JESUS! Again, Nunny? She's at it again! Faceless fuck *du jour.* She was "Mommy" when I was younger and naive and would cover my ears with the musty skirt of a Holly Hobby doll that I stole from the Salvation Army. Holly Hobby was just some hippie-looking saint of a girl that looked like a nurturing pal. I look at her now, all soft, stained and fraying, covered with suburban grime and think: '70s casualty. She can't offer me anything anymore.

Sweet, Jesus! I never cover my ears anymore. *Oh Father! Father!* It all makes me stronger. She calls all of her dates, "Father." Keep your voice down.

The holy cross is cut a little off center from my licorice main vein, decorating both of my inner wrists. I've decided the subtle approach can work just fine. I call it my attempt at minimalism. *Yessss.* I wonder who it is this time. I play with tiny crispy flaps of skin as if they weren't mine. Such a decadent habit, yes, I am aware. Just like now I am aware that the art of it is secondary to the feeling I enjoy so much. *Ohhhhhhhh.* My veins have orgasms. That's the only explanation I have for the blood rushing out of the wound that way. I love to de-virginize unmarked skin territory. Epidermal hymen, if you will.

I pick some skin out from under my index finger and chew on it. *Ohhhhhhhhhhhhh.*

She just won't quit.

Scenes of a Family

The Stage is bare to convey the bareness of their existence.

SCENE I. LISHA'S *Bedroom. A door slams. Footsteps are heard. In walks* JENNY, LISHA'S *younger sister.* JENNY *is a striking young babe who has the appearance of innocence, but if one looks very deeply into her eyes, one can tell that she is fucked up or over. She wears clothing that is inexpensively fashionable...however not as gutter-influenced as* LISHA'S. *They both make do with what they can find at thrift stores in the city.*

JENNY: Hey Lish. Tired! Orchestra rehearsal again. *(She tosses her viola case on her bed and flops down next to* LISHA.*)* I need your help with this project of mine.

LISHA *(yawning and turning the pages of* Love and Rockets*)*: Nunny the whore is at it again.

JENNY *(so lost little girl...)*: Huh?

LISHA: I thought they'd come through the fucking floor.

JENNY: Aww, come on.

LISHA: What priest is she fucking this time? *(She fidgets with her sleeves.)*

JENNY *(blind, blind, blind!)*: You know that kind of thing doesn't go on anymore.

LISHA: Uhh, yeah, right, sure, good, great. *(The words come out in a rush.)*

JENNY: God, just stop freaking me out.

LISHA *(jumping on the bed and wildly flailing her arms, Viking Girl with a spear, sings gaily)*: Wake up, little Sissy, wake up. Er er er er er.

JENNY *(tries, but fails, to be flip)*: Hey, are you at it

again with butchering yourself?

LISHA: Save it sissy. You do your viola thing and I don't rag on you. This is my thing. Besides, if you had to hear what I had to hear before...

JENNY (*giggles like such a girl*): I'd just play my viola! (*Lisha pretends to violently, but eloquently, puke.*)

(*A knock is heard on the door and almost immediately the girls' mother, NUNNY, walks in, wearing a kimono-type robe. She looks euphoric and Long Island trash. Her church mien, the look she typically employs, is as vanished as her bra. This is clearly not the woman most of the neighbors know and pretend to love because she overcame her socio-economic disadvantages and made daily visits to church.*)

NUNNY: Girls, I got news. First give your mutha a kiss. (*JENNY walks over in a rote fashion and does so without hesitating, but LISHA visibly recoils.*) What the hell is your problem? Got ya curse or something?

LISHA: I'm not kissing a mouth just got back from fellating, *ma mere.*

NUNNY: I don't know what you're talking about. But anyway...

LISHA: Yeah, yeah, yeah, yeahhhhhh...

NUNNY: Will you shut up for a change! Girls, listen to this...

LISHA: Get the hell on with it, already. (*Under her breath.*) It probably sucks anyway.

NUNNY: Ya mutha's getting married! Well? Congratulate me for Christ's sake!

JENNY (*controlled*): We're happy for you, Mom. (*She hugs her and leaves the room.*)

LISHA *(yells out after her)*: Speak for yourself, Sissy, there ain't no "we" in this equation. *(To* NUNNY, *and so casual, it kills.)* Was it the guy you were just fucking, by any chance?

NUNNY: What the hell are ya talking about, ya little ungrateful, obnoxious brat? Goddammit, I don't ask for much, just for my dawtas to be a little happy for me. And to help me out a bit here. After all the crap I've done for yous...

LISHA: Well, *ya* ain't getting diddley fucking *squat* from me, woman.

NUNNY: Show some respect, dammit. I'll give ya a smack. You're not too old.

LISHA: Respect? What the hell do you think *Christ* called his Mother?

NUNNY: Don't ya dare put your blasphemous ass in the same league as my Lord.

LISHA: I'm outta here. Oh, when's the date, just so I know? Not that I care...

NUNNY: November Second. All Soul's Day. *(Adds graciously for some stupid reason.)* And yiz both will be my maids a hona. Tell your sista. You both gotta organize my party.

LISHA *(somewhat maliciously)*: Will you wear white?

(LISHA *exits like a maniac doing a Balanchine ballet.*)

November the second. Mexico's Day of the Dead celebration. The possibilities are so inspiring and endless that I'm no longer in Long Island, but over there, south of the border. I think my services are needed at this affair. Hell, expected even, my being maid of honor, or whatever the fuck.

Day of the Dead. In the American Catholic Church we have the insipid services for All Souls' Day. I like how the Mexicans fuck the euphemism of "souls." The *Dead*. That's it, man.

They are welcoming back and embracing their dead. Toy skeletons are everywhere. Baby Jesus skeletons. Skeletons waiting tables. Puppet skeletons playing instruments. Papier-mâché skeletons in coffins. Pastel sugared skulls for the children. Bride and groom skeletons. The altars are strewn with candles, candy and flowers. Death is more than violets. It's marigolds, purple cockscomb, baby's breath—dead, dying, alive, just picked-all to symbolize the process. Their flowery stench permeates the air to welcome the souls, to repel the evil spirits. Candles the only light and a little old man's shadow looks grotesquely large on the wall behind him as he prays in front of the shrine. Death is decadent, sultry and vibrant. Tomb and gravesite areas laden with sugared skeletons and flowers, resplendent with offerings, a bottle of tequila, perhaps.

Let's change channels for a moment: Long Island, the land of the depraved, privileged, and decadent=decay. The stench of decay is not destroyed by the fresh flowers. The Wedding Ritual: dance-eat-schmooze-clink glasses to elicit kissing—admire dresses *(can you believe the dress on that one)*. The clichéd ice sculpture of two doves and a heart. (Gag—how about two skeletons embracing? Daunting enough?) Piles of food like exterminated rodents. Abundance of abundance of...love...future...the show...bride appearing in a puff of smoke—lowered by a flowered trapeze—popping out of a mini castle. The bride is queen. And it's all *mise-en-scène*.

SCENE II. *Two days later.* JENNY *and* LISHA'S *bedroom. In the background, moaning and various spiritual ecstasies are heard.*

JENNY *(sadly, and so like a wee-wee):* I hate hearing Mom.

LISHA: Hallelujah! She finally acknowledges Nunny the whore.

JENNY: Stop being so cool about it. *(Waaah.)*

LISHA: So, how should I be? I've faced the facts for years now.

JENNY *(as usual, avoids a confrontation):* How many do you think she's had?

LISHA: Well, I could tell you, but I'm not sure you can deal with such a situation, you might just walk out or something.

JENNY *(such a wuss):* Oh, come on, Lish, what could I do, really? Her choice has nothing to do with us.

LISHA: Yeah, right. Nothing. That's why you should have given her no reaction. Like you don't give a shit. Like me.

JENNY: You...

LISHA: Yes. Learn to be impassive. It drives her nuts. You looked *hurt*, for God's sake.

JENNY *(looking down):* I mean, I haven't even met the guy.

LISHA: Exactly. Because it has nothing to do with us. She wants us all happy and shit for her. Gag. I won't play that game.

(Enter NUNNY *as a sun expecting her daughter planets to revolve around her.)*

NUNNY: So, girls, what are yiz wearing?

LISHA *(looking down at her clothes, a gorgeous ensemble)*: Looks like a pink t-shirt with a black fishnet bodysuit underneath, black miniskirt, green tights, boots...*(Yes, she does look that cool.)*

NUNNY: Don't get fresh with me, missy. Yiz know what I mean. For my big day. Your gowns...

JENNY *(hastily)*: Whatever you want, Mom.

NUNNY *(getting pissed)*: I'm asking *yiz*. If I had any idears I wouldn't be asking, would I?

JENNY: Well, I was thinking, since we're broke, maybe I could wear the dress I wore to the junior prom last year. It's the only thing formal I got.

NUNNY: Naw. Y'ain't wearing that old thing for my wedding, for Christ's sake. You'll be walking down the aisle in Church for everyone to see—what'll they think? You'll buy a new dress. You can save money by missing the school trip to that stupid Broadway play. That's fifty bucks right there. Make yourself lunch in the mornings from now on and don't go out next weekend. There—ya got a dress now, don't you?

LISHA *(gasping with glee)*: Oh goody! Can I also sacrifice my eating habits and social life for the next week and a half so that I can buy a new dress for your oh-so-important wedding, too? I've got a stylin' sleeveless black frock in mind...

NUNNY: Sleeveless? Are you fuckin' crazy? You gonna cover up those damned arms or I'll chop them off.

JENNY *(Horrified at NUNNY'S callousness)*: Mom!

NUNNY: They look like they've been gnawed on by some rat in the house instead of that so-called "cat" of yours. *(Grumbles to herself.)* Have people think we got some rodents in the house. *(As usual only giving a fuck about what neighbors and parishioners think. To say nothing of her priestly acquaintances.)*

JENNY: Lisha, she's just being up to her cruel stuff. Don't take her seriously. Tell her you don't mean it, Mom.

LISHA *(momentarily surprised that* NUNNY *has even noticed, then visibly hardened as a Viking again)*: I'm wearing what I want if you want me to go.

NUNNY: Yeah, so everyone can see my looney dawta. Not if I can help it. I think what you need is to see Father Frank.

LISHA: Is he one of those you brought up to your room? *(She laughs. As usual one up on her dimwit mother.)*

NUNNY *(spits at her)*: Get out of my sight, you little bitch.

*(*LISHA *calmly walks out.* JENNY *is on the verge of tears.)*

Here's one. Jenny *loves* her mother. Oh, *yes*. She can't help it, she says. She and I grew up together, but I've felt nothing but indifference towards our Nunny since I was a child. No, since I was aware of things around me, which probably goes back to when I was a baby.

Jenny says she doesn't ever want to be like her mother. A slut of a nun who got the fist and fled. It was only that one time with Billy, she said. But she's fist-less and free now. Thanks to me.

My baby sister. Little girl with mud coming out of her mouth like spit or drool. Little girl giggling at Mommy's palms when she held them out for us to admire. Jenny would always mistake the blood for a treat. She'd run up and lick them both. *It's sweet*, she would squeal. I just stood there outside and stared down the sun. To me it was like God or something,.

Sweet. (gasp) *Fucking.* (gasp) *Jesus.* At it again. It must be "love." He's gotta be loaded. Why else would she settle down with just one, when she has enjoyed scores? She didn't introduce him. She never does. Thinks we don't know what she's doing in there. Prayer group or perhaps an exorcism.

Sweeeeet, ohhh. I've heard it all. I see her sometimes sneaking them in when she thinks we're busy in our room, or out. Some arcane operation. A *priest service*, perhaps? I swear one guy chanted something in Latin as he came. Nunny may be a whore to priests but at least she's protecting some child who'd otherwise be the unwilling recipient. In fact, that's the only thing that keeps me from blowing the lid off the entire operation. Mom is just a receptacle. Ruined. Jenny and I are her products—however, we both have potential to do better in life.

SCENE III. *That bedroom. The two goddesses are doing their homework (sort of...)*

JENNY (*employing her best mooch voice*): Lisha, genius, I need your help with something. An English paper on rituals or something.

LISHA (*looks up from a new book she's into at the moment, probably de Sade, or Joyce*): I would help you—

JENNY: But—

LISHA: But I'm not sure you could handle this precarious

situation. You might walk out, or cry or something.

JENNY: What are you talking about? This is my home-work, now.

LISHA: Sure, that's what it seems like, but it's really part of a much larger issue, isn't it?

JENNY *(whine, whine, WHINE)*: I hate issues! That's a Lisha thing.

LISHA: Okay, whatever. Just keep up the front with me. And I know I'm saying this for like the millionth time, why the fuck should we care about her?

JENNY: I don't know. I guess she's sort of our mother.

LISHA: Sort of a mother...Yeah, she lent us her womb to grow in. Big whoop. *Mother*. It's in name only. Does a plant owe a garden, technically? No less, care about it.

JENNY *(buh bye issue)*: Are you going to help me, or not? We have to take care of the wedding reception as well, or should I say *I do*, I'm sure you're not into it.

LISHA: Hey, don't count on that. Hell, yeah you've got a deal, I'll even do both "projects," on one condition.

JENNY: Yeah?

LISHA: I look at both as creative outlets, opportunities, if you will. Are you able to utilize artistic license on this essay?

JENNY: Meaning?

LISHA: Meaning expanding on the topic. Make it a pro-ject instead of a mere essay. A play posing as an essay, and then the visuals presented on film as the grand finale.

JENNY: Sounds good to me.

Nunny's day is coming soon. *Dia de los Muertes*. Mexi-cans embrace their dead children. *Angelitos*, they call them. Little angels. Ashen children shrouded in white wraps. Oh, yes, I'm going all out for this one. Nunny deserves it. She used to try to instill those good Xian values to Jenny and I. Jenny is still somewhat brainwashed, but I got over the Catholic jive eons ago when I was a kid and realized so much of that shit I learned in CCD just didn't make sense. In the colorful books that talked about being a good Xian I'd see these happy, photogenic families that did not exist in my world. They'd appear surrounding a dinner table, heads bowed before a well-balanced meal, or holding hands and smiling on the way to church (I'd be dragged by Nunny, kicking and screaming). Then we'd have the smiling, non-threatening Jesus in a connect-the-dots. What the hell was that for, anyway?

I was forced to participate in this fraudulent "education," though. I didn't go quietly. Fuck, I even made my confirmation. My good Nunny Pie saw to it that I did all of it. How would it look for her, an ex-nun, to have such a sacrilegious daughter? But I got her back, picking the name Lilith as my confirmation name. There wasn't a damn thing she could do about it, because it's a Biblical name, but man, did it piss her off.

Lisha, in a long white robe with red piping along the edges. A lengthy procession of her pious peers, all set to take their vows. Snooze, snooze, snooze, all in a row. Then she heard it. Pricked up her ears. The magic word. "Do you reject Satan and all his works..." "Nooo! I luuuv bloody Satan! *God is dead! Satan lives! Hail Satan Hail Satan Hail Satan Hail Satan...*" The rest of the kids joined in and we became the geriatric cult members of *Rosemary's Baby*.

Later on at home I caught the Mom-as-Martyr treatment. Oh, the wailing and fainting. Oh, oh, oh.

She didn't get the gag. For about a week I was forced to sleep with candles and incense burning around a malevolent picture of Christ. Every hour more blood poured from His eyes. I got sick of it and bought a picture of the angel of death to put in *her* fucking room. It freaked her out momentarily, but then she forced the stigmata on me. I woke up with it, but I knew it was her doing. That night she must have slipped me something in my almond milk before I went to sleep. She only thought she won.

But it's Lisha's time now.

SCENE IV. *Two days before the wedding.* LISHA *and* JENNY *are yet again sequestered in their bedroom.*

JENNY: How's it coming, Lisha?
LISHA: It's nothing less than brilliant, actually. Need you even ask?
JENNY *(grumbles)*: Of course not. It *is* my midterm though.
LISHA: Oh, but it's so much more than a mere midterm, let me tell you, Sissy.

(A knock at the door. Without even the decency of waiting for a response, NUNNY *stomps in, in full flouncy ho mode, all breathy and kimonoed.)*

LISHA: What the fuck? Can't you ever put those fists to good use?
NUNNY *(brightly)*: Ignoring! *(Breathes dramatically.)* Finally yiz both are here.
LISHA: Getting histrionic on us again?

NUNNY: I'm fine, what the hell are you talking about?

LISHA: Out with it already. Stop wasting our time with your nonsense.

NUNNY (*grandly, with her usual over-estimated degree of self-importance*): I have a surprise for yiz, my loving dawtas.

JENNY (*weak as ever, who cares?*): Oh, what Mom?

LISHA: Uh, let me guess, hmm, you've decided to continue being a hooker even after you get married to keep the cash flowing!

NUNNY: Ya asking for it, Freak Girl! Normally, you know what you'd get for that one, but (*LISHA braces herself for the cliché.*) I'm in love and I'm happy, so I'll just ignore it and present to you...my fiancé, Greggy.

(*JENNY attempts a grin, but LISHA whoops it up, cheering with exaggerated excitement and jumps from her bed to JENNY'S. NUNNY, so typically delusional, thinks that she's actually sincere.*)

NUNNY: Hold ya horses. Shit. Ya'd think I was introducing some new way to kill yourself, or something. (*Looks behind her, realizing her prize hasn't yet materialized.*) Greggy, where the hell are ya, Baby?

(*GREGGY appears, and in the grand tradition of white trash, he is visibly younger than her and quite a dude, looks-wise, that is. She pulls him in through the door, where he is faltering. It is so damn obvious that he is her Muppet.*)

LISHA (*leaps off the bed to appraise him*): Yep. "Baby" is right. Which of your friend's tits did you pull him off of?

JENNY *(tersely)*: Hi.

NUNNY: That's Jenny there. That's my flower.

LISHA: And I'm her weed, man, what's up?

GREGGY *(clueless)*: Weed? Flower? I don't get it. Huh huh. *(Duh.)*

NUNNY: Lisha, get away from my man, you slut. Yeah, I see ya circling him like he's your prey.

GREGGY *(attempts at a laugh. Oh, he has "dork" and "bonehead" not to mention "doormat" written all over his stud-boy visage)*: Uh, chill, Chrissy.

NUNNY: Now sweetie, it isn't your business what I say to my dawtas, is it?

GREGGY *(clearly whipped to shreds)*: Sorry, honey.

So he isn't a priest, it turns out. Just a log roller, or some other sort of job with hands-on implications. And the ripped bod to match. He is such a toy for her. Brawny and brainless. I've always said, a man is useless when he doesn't have a tangible brain and that accounts for about half of them. I actually can't hate him, but I feel sorry for the dude. He was all, "nice to meet yous" to Jenny and I in that stupid Long Island stud boy way. I think he may even try to open up a bagel shop of his own some day. Well, I can see why she makes so much noise, now. But in the past it was to put on the act for the holy fathers. Earlier yet, it was for *The* Father, or so she fooled herself into believing.

Lisha as a child hears her mother's wails. She is curious and goes to her Nunny's room to find the source. Her Nunny, there on the bed writhing and screaming. Two stern men standing at the bedposts robed in black. She, writhing for His glory. Lisha backs out, and runs out of the house as if she is sanity herself and hides in the woods down the street, scraping at her palms until they bleed for real. Later in life, at a different time and place, Nunny Pie would come to explain to her daughter the cause of her orgiastic feast. *Stigmata darling. See ya ma's palms? That's for the Lord Jesus.* She wanted Lisha to lick them, but she refused, preferring her own, of course.

SCENE V. *A couple of hours later.* GREGGY *is sitting at the table like a Long Island god, drinking a beer, legs apart, taking up as much space as a human animal is capable of, or maybe staking his claim yo! as a MAN.* LISHA *innocently walks by and sees this as an opportunity to grill him like a marinated vegetable.*

LISHA *(decides to employ a subtle Long Island accent to put him at ease)*: Hi, Greggy. What's with the Heiny? Bud, now that's a real *man's* beer!

GREGGY: Heineken is my beer, and I am a man. *(Generally jigsawed.)*

LISHA: Uh, yeah. Whatever. I'm into them 40s myself!

GREGGY: Forty what?

LISHA: Oh, you know, OE, Colt 45 and a coupla friends.

GREGGY: Huh?

LISHA: Uh, forget it, all right. So, *yiz* are getting married, huh?

GREGGY: Yep. Me and your Mom.

LISHA: Catholic?

GREGGY *(seems shocked that she should even ask)*: Of course!

LISHA: Me too. Sucks, right?

GREGGY: No. I would never say that. I go to church

every Sunday. It's how I met your mom.

LISHA *(feels ill, but decides to cut right to the chase)*: Do you reject Satan and the glamour of evil?

GREGGY: Huh? Satan?

LISHA: You heard me, boy. Answer the question.

GREGGY: I mean, what kind of question is that? Of course I despise Satan. I never was even into heavy metal for Christ's sake. Oops, I mean...

LISHA: Save it for Nunny, Greggy, or shall I call you Kermit? *(She knows this guy isn't for real. He probably doesn't even know the Lord's Prayer. Something is fishy on the Muppet Show.)*

GREGGY: Wait! I didn't want to offend you by taking the Lord's name in vain.

LISHA: Listen man, whatever. You're useless to me if she has that much influence on you. *(Mockingly.)* I will pray for you my son.

GREGGY: God bless you.

LISHA: Oh, don't even. I didn't sneeze. You're dismissed, soldier.

(GREGGY walks down the hall back to NUNNY'S control pad, head down. LISHA pours his piss water down the sink.)

I have this chick donating the use of her camcorder. She'll have to record when I walk down the aisle. I guess I'm willing to relinquish control for that. Nunny left the decorating up to Jenny, her favorite child, of course. Nunny has no clue that I am so immersed in this aspect of her life. I am directing this scene. The camcorder is to record the blissful event for Jenny's school project, as well as for my own personal library.

Now I'm on my way to peruse the local funeral parlors, for the last important touch.

Angelica

She lays out in front of me, her head engulfed in the pastel blue cloud of the pillow, its edges laced with white. She wears a white dress trimmed with yellow daisies. She wears a white face. She wears white arms and legs and hands, but not her neck—it wears white, is halo'd with red blotches, a candy cane. Her face reads peace but with a violent violet, beautiful as hell in hell never never never in hell. Her body knows a soft cloudy context. She grasps a bouquet in her fists. She even smells sweet. An incorruptible. Angelica. I lift you and you are so heavy. A small dense animal.

Yet another important occasion in my short life has arrived. Sometimes I feel as though I spend most of my time nowadays thriving on such occasions. There's nothing much to live for in between.

Jenny is still at home upstairs, frocking herself out. Nunny could be engaging in some pre-marital fornication with her Muppet, for all I know. There are more important matters to take care of now. I make a quick stop at the Knights of Columbus hall where I've set up the reception. The room is bare of all your clichéd wedding bullshit. Instead, I've created a make-shift cemetery festooned as the cemeteries in Mexico would be on this day.

*Here comes the bride...*Tombs instead of tables. Random flowers in all stages from life to death instead of ostentatious expensive arrangements. The decorations—mirthful death masks, candles. The food—sugar skulls and death bread, tamales, and some tofu tacos thrown in for good measure. The favors are a surprise. I know that even if at first the guests go away shocked and disturbed, it'll force some deep thoughts into their heads. A figurative assault.

I'm already dressed for the occasion, choosing a costume keeping up with the theme. I'm wearing a Victorian dress of mourning, but I've sculpted a death mask out of silk threads and wire that I plan to hold over my face, so that I look like a Day of the Dead toy. *Day of the Dead* has come.

Ex-nuns can't get married in a church (besides, what priest would even want to *go there?*), so the ceremony is about to take place in just over an hour in this hall that is most definitely in cahoots with the church. Fifty of Nunny's closest friends were invited. Everything is set, now all I have to do is wait. I burn the incense so my Angelica can thrill in the aromas. So she can come back to me here.

The room is full of pained, forced smiles. Maybe they can see through Nunny's facade at long last. The visual aids. Stimuli they cannot ignore. There is a child here. Everyone who is present has met her through a wedding favor photograph. In it, I, embracing Angelica, stare straight through them all, as I do in real life. I hand the photos out one by one to the guests as they arrive. Now they try to keep their eyes peeled on Nunny's procession.

The guests are oohing and aahing over Nunny's "tasteful" (read *no attempt at expressing the possibility of born-again virginity*) lilac lace dress. A few people have dropped the pictures of Angelica and they flutter like dying butterflies to the floor. Their fingers flutter too, a careless dance. Ignoring, ignored, all eyes on the bride. She's all that matters now. Her sloe eyes are fixed reverently on the priest, who is also enthralled with the picture of pristine brideliness. Greggy is waiting with a vapid smile.

Vows in hushed tones—I don't even pay attention. Angelica is all I can think of. She was dressed in a special gown, too, infinitely more ravishing in death than this woman before me in the ecclesiastic ceremony she's frauding her way through. I wait for some reaction from the guests, but their eyes hold nothing but the whore in bride's clothing.

SCENE VI. *Knights of Columbus Hall. The ceremony is finished. The reception is about to commence.* LISHA *approaches* NUNNY *who is obviously anxious to schmooze it up with the guests.*

LISHA: Nunny, oh Nunny! Have some time for your loving daughter. *(Now all eyes are on the two of them...show show show!)*
NUNNY *(grins like the superior show chick she is)*: Of course honey, what is it?
LISHA: Don't you love my decorating job? Let's hear.
NUNNY: Of course, sweetie, you know I do. It's just lovely, right folks? (LISHA *is shocked to see the guests nod their agreement.)*
GUEST #1: Mexican is so *in* this year besides. And of course, it's very respectful to take into consideration All Soul's Day. What a good Catholic girl you are. Just lovely. I can't wait to dig into some of those tamales!
LISHA *(oh goody!)*: And the favors?

NUNNY *(still has no idea)*: Oh, yes, just what I had in mind.

GUEST #1: And what a novel idea to have your daughter's picture!

NUNNY *(Delighted?? What a Streep!)*: Oh, yes. *(Confused.)* And now I would like to discuss the food with my lovely daughter. Come here, Honey. (LISHA *and her* NUNNY *go off to the ladies room.)*

NUNNY: Just what the hell do ya mean, trying to steal the show that way? Uh uh. This is my wedding. You have no right. What the hell will people think? I'm going to go off now to delight my guests. Try to stay out of the picture, you hear me? *(Shouts to her adoring fans:)* Yes, don't you just love the Mexican theme? I told Lisha just what to do. Feel free to take the decorations home.

LISHA *(to the viewers)*: And the moral of the story is...people have no morals, much less decency. Let's hear it for family values!

The End

It's all over except for the clean up, which I am loath to do. I will not until I see my Angelica once more. I stare at her picture and by doing this I hope to look up then and see her apparition before me like a flash of ghost lightning. Then She will grasp me and erase my scars because She has died for my sins, but not by my hands which created them. I wait for you in this cemetery garden with candle flowers, their flames, the bud which I, acting as bee, will soon suck into my own...flesh.

She will be saved.
She will save.

Stains

I FEEL ALL SORTS OF THINGS THESE DAYS (the fingers, like the legs of a tarantula, multiply continuously, but nowhere to be seen, tickling creeping forcing terror so that I can feel it everywhere soon, my waist my toes the insides of my thighs). It all began with going back to the closet again last week.

Going Back

Sometimes my sense of accomplishment can come from something as mundane as the act of cleaning up. Memorabilia is an impetus.

I find a piece of paper in the closet. "Lisha is me. Jenny is my sister. Devon is my best friend. My hobbies are putting on makeup, saving poor animals from mean people, and I love to play with babies. My favorite things are Pippi Longstocking, firecrackers, bubblegum, *Kissing Potion* and the Lord." The page is crumpled in my second grade religion book, which is stuffed in the corner of my closet under shoe boxes, scarves, flip-flop sandals, Jenny's old viola, and a picture of Jesus against a red velvet curtain.

I used to like "The Lord." There it is in crooked handwriting, in blue ink, on white paper.

I can see the family portrait that year, as painted by Salvador Dali: the Son in my palms, the Father in my veil, the Holy Spirit in Jenny's mouth, and Nunny looming over us, the Blessed Mother of the backyard mud garden.

First Holy Communion: May 14, 1979. But something obliterates the picture that I see in my mind. (It's like you come from out of nowhere. You come back to me. You remember me. I don't need to leave for a while.)

I am existing in the world of the closet now.

In the Closet a Few Months Ago

A few days after freeing Jenny from her fist in this very closet, I was putting all the stuff back inside. The clothes, the jackets, the old toys, and the notebooks— first through eleventh grade. I sorted through the pages, which were all stained for assorted reasons: orange juice from a winter breakfast in first grade; coffee from a spring breakfast in eighth grade; blood from a skin design in eleventh grade. Then I found another sort of stain near the left corner of the closet towards the back. A hard to reach spot, so I must have missed it when I cleaned up afterwards. It was right then I felt it for the first time—I tried to ignore it, but it was there—a long finger pointing in my lower back and next it slowly dragged its way—curiously—to my neck and then over the back of my head to the top and then my face. I got up and went looking for a sponge.

And now, I need to get out of the closet. That finger may be back again.

Phone Conversation with Devon

"Hey what's that screaming in the background?"

"It's Siouxsie. The new one," I say, first thing that comes to mind.

"Oh, no wonder."

Something grabs me from behind; all I can feel is its hands. *(You?!)*

"Can you come over for a little while?" I manage to ask.

"Some other time, Lish. I have to call Nick. We may hang out. It's been ages."

"And that's a bad thing? That self-promoting unctuous psychopath. Why don't you tell him to get over himself. He's not the only lunatic to have graced the shores of Long Island."

"Hey, that's my guy you're dissing. I've told you a million times why his schizo head is a major turn on. Look, I'm done with this, Lish. Later."

Bitch. Some friend.

In Bed

All of the lights out in the room, except for the one in the closet. Waking, I realize I am immobile, surrounded by a beguiling cloud and all at once it's the fingers.

(You're at me and I am helpless. I grunt with a confused anguish and you are enjoying yourself, aren't you?) The Uncurled Fist. I lay supine, a layer of fingered flesh on the bed. You have left your stain—I have the colors to prove it, blue and yellow. You're the burnt smell that always accompanies your presence. I remember you—almost liquid on the floor of the closet.

You seemed so harmless that way—a liquid lunch. You could have been food to a starving creature then, but I quickly cleaned up. This is the thanks I get.

So now I lie on top of the covers awake through the assault. The burning seeps its way into my nose and at the same time, I feel it upon my flesh. Your fingers first prod—then poke—then burn my flesh. Payback is hard. You perceive my nascent groaning. It excites you because you know your advantage when I'm down. You move even faster, even more relentlessly. Curl back into the fist. I can take a punch better.)

Jenny stays asleep. She doesn't know her fist is on its own. And it doesn't blame her at all. It's at me. The fingers have found *me*.

Little Guy Butterfly

But no, wait.

He had been born a moribund butterfly. Wings with millions of microscopic feathers, so fragile so soft so boneless, to paralyze with a touch. And he fell out or I dropped him. I can't remember (I *did* care about you once. At the time I was just so anxious for things to go right).

I can see this child has grown to be a child genius. My nephew. I dropped him and he moves forever clumsily, his brain stunted, but he's a savant.

Think of a butterfly. When it is on the ground, it is no longer graceful, is it? People only think of butterflies as *graceful*, because they are so beautiful. Beauty and grace forever go hand in hand off into the sunset like Diana the Huntress and her bow. In truth, of course, butterflies can barely fly straight without bumping into something, and are so easily caught in a child's net. And when they are touched, they can never fly again.

My Little Guy Butterfly, he is beautiful, and he likes to twirl string—he is positively mesmerized by it—that he grasps between his feelers. He can memorize subway maps, as well, so I have supplied with him the maps of subways all around the world.

He amazes people in this way. He can tell people how to get almost anywhere in the world! It works like this: he asks a person—he always writes it down; he will not speak—*What did you do last night?* The person answers, *Went to the city. Caught a movie.* They expect it to end right then and there, but it never does. *Where, what street. Tell me the street.* He writes this fumbling with the pencil and paper, but compulsively, to get it out. *The Quad on...the Quad,* he is already writing so they stop, *the Quad on 13th, between Fifth and Sixth Avenues, take the F to 14th or the N and R, 4, 5, and 6 to Union Square.* And then, the person is puzzled, looks to me, *Isn't he?* And I slowly shake my head, smiling. They never believe it at first. Then slowly but surely as they get to know him, they realize. They are most shocked when he gives advice for sightseeing in cities like London, Moscow and Paris. Amazing isn't he? That's my Little Guy. All this at the tender age of 6. He even amazes me sometimes, and I am truly hard to amaze! I am so damn lucky to have him, so lucky the abortion was aborted. Otherwise he would be nothing more than a stain on the floor of the closet.

Something Happens at School During the Day

I'm at my desk, doodling designs of butterflies drawn to

a light bulb, except they are burning the tips of their wings, those little baby feathers that the eye cannot perceive.

And then I feel *them*. Now. Why now when I'm at school? Indeed, why not? They specifically choose my ears and mouth, but not my eyes, so I can see everyone staring at me like my teacher just asked me a question, including the teacher, so I guess she did. I can't do a damn thing, except look like some emulating fan of Helen Keller.

My orifices are all awfully raw, so off to the Powder. Its fingers are guiding me from behind and that's how I get there. I'm not sure yet if I want to kiss them or break them. They are thumping an infuriating rhythm, a furious laughter. The lights are so strong in here, I fear for my skin. And suddenly they disappear. And *he's* in here. The butterfly has overcome the fingers of the fist. Either that or they just don't feel like fucking with us at this point in time. Thump thump thump. It's *him* I hear. What are you doing here, Little Guy? Go find Mommy. Thump slide thump thump thump.

He is so goddamned adorable. Little Guy graceful with his twisted and limp limbs. He learned to adapt, make more of himself than expected. He's in school even, way ahead of his time—must be all that subway map memorization. He leaves without looking at me. (Why did you lead him to the Powder?) He was embarrassed and he left and now I have no butterfly. No Little Guy, but the fingers are back. I have to piss when I'm nervous, so I go in a stall to do so, because I sure as hell cannot control it...and they are "helping me." I force myself to laugh in the fingers of fear, because it sure isn't any help having fingers stroke your kidneys and bladder when you're nervous and you're trying to piss. Why do they always know right where to go? I pull up my pants because I can't go under these conditions, I sure can't. Like a fucking UTI. So, I'll just grin, bear it, and think of the Little Guy Butterfly.

Fingered

Every night for the past week or so, I am being fingered inveterately in bed, intermittently during the day (just enough so that I can function while looking like a complete spazoid at times). Someone else could say, painfully so, but I don't. I'm saying that convincingly: *I don't.*

There are enough fingers so that my every orifice can be filled; for every one I think I remove there are two to take its place. I learned the hard way, so now I don't fight it. Now I just allow the fingers of the fist to patiently give me my due (until I agree with you: yeah, I deserve all of it and it will only serve to make me stronger. Maybe someday, I will swallow you whole without choking). The fingers fluctuate with their intent—to violate—to stimulate—to tantalize…or is it I who is undecided in how to interpret their intentions? The fist was definitely male, but the fingers of the fist are a different story. They are androgynous because they are caught between testosterone torture and the feminine nurturing caress. I like the caress much less. I hate being left vulnerable and unprepared.

Maybe I'm totally off base here. What the hell is a caress, anyway?

Flutter Flutter

Little Guy, my little pie, let Auntie make it up to you? He mouths, *I'm fine.*

Mouth full of treat. No, you're not, little guy, see you dropped it and you have strawberry ice cream all over your face and shirt. I will feed it to you, little guy.

He mouths, *no.* Then that tortured throat sound-slash-groan that always kills me. He doesn't talk much, but there are a lot of interesting sounds coming from him. Clash thump thump.

I feel he is bursting with all sorts of potential. His feet flop on the floor doing a clumsy swan-like choreography while he tries to get to the floor to pick up the spoon. I do it for him. First I wash the ice cream out of his nose. Then I feed him with the spoon. Here come the fingers dancing all over me in the correct balletic manner. The fingers are always triumphant when Little Guy fails. (what are you trying to tell me with this? There you are all smug, trying to destroy the *self,* had you grown to fruition.

There you are, trying to trip—to dance—to flip him like a fried butterfly so you can grease your fingers and facilitate things; you want to be slippery and slip into the tightest orifices). *Th-th-th-eee*, he stutters. He speaks! *Yes, mine Butterfly, the what? Ffffff-ingggg. Don't pay them any mind. No one else can feel them but you and I. No one else cares. I'm sorry. No one else is around, Little Guy.* And he cries. So do I. He envelopes me with his fluttering wings and then I recognize what a caress truly is.

Jenny = A Mom

(Do you ever visit *her?* She was your mother, after all. No, no, probably only me. Only my act was the cause of your burn, your meltdown.) What I want to know is, does Jenny realize the light bulb has continuously been slowly burning out ever since? Does this freak her the fuck out? I doubt it. I doubt it has even the minutest effect on her. (Do you feel sorry for her? Is that it? What did it for you? Was it the way she screamed due to you punching her on your way out? Was it the seizure—the thrashing—the wailing—her obvious reluctance to give you the rake? Do you think I made her do it? Trust me, it was too late to go back at that point. I only helped her along. But where is she anyway? Can you find her?)

Food Is Repulsive, but Milkshakes Are Glee

Now for the first time, I can't keep the food down. At night, the fingers have gotten in the habit to go down my throat to force the food back up, and I make sure not to eat after 5 p.m. so I can get at least a few hours of sleep at night. But it's not enough.

Sometimes I can't help it, and scarf down something that won't kill on the way up and out. Peanut butter is a definite no-no. Water is a definite *yes* every night before bedtime. That comes up like my esophagus is any old sink pipe. If I take nothing, then it's the bile. So thick and orange, making permanent stains on the sheets. The smear of my sins!

Lunchtime can be a battle, though. I've taken to eating alone in a secluded place, sharing with Little Guy what I cannot put in my mouth due to the fingers deciding to play "keep away" with me (when he is present, you can hardly be. I choose to feed him, rather than satisfy *you* with my purging). I guess losing a few pounds wouldn't kill me. Hell, the undernourished look is always a hit in Long Island fast food establishments where overweight JAPs and Guidettes give me hungry glares as I sail by with loads of french fries on my tray, to be washed down gleefully with thick shakes. How could they know it'll probably never get the chance to reach my gut? Little Guy may get half when the other half winds up on the chipped brown wall. He just loves milkshakes. Just loves the opportunity for sweets, one of his great joys in life. I gently tip the thick paper cup towards his fluttering lips which are barely there, but *I* can see them. His eyes are pure wonder; I love to look deep into them. Pure black, no white anywhere, and shiny as wet stones, but then they are usually teary. He can't help it and this way I can never forget that it's my fault; all is my fault. So I give him milkshakes, pour gradually until the brain is joyfully numbed by the cold sweetness and the wet eyes are frozen as if his face is right under the surface of a winter lake, still; always beseeching me, his aunt.

Clunk Thump Thump

He's seven now and the pride of the family. When he's on a car ride he mouths the names of the street signs and house addresses. He has a bright future. He could write more effective maps for any metropolitan area in the country. The world, even. But he still needs constant care, otherwise. I'm there to give it to him. He thinks he is independent, but I know he needs me.

Jenny could care less. Sometimes he thump-thump-fumbles over to her. Does she notice? Not a chance. There's a begging butterfly look in his eyes, Sis. And she keeps practicing on that damn viola like he's not even there. Like she can't even hear his clanking leg braces over the racket of her instrument. He doesn't speak, still, so he can't yell at her, but he does make sounds. He falls on purpose, I think, to get her attention, but never gets it. And then he just lies there fluttering, crippled butterfly on the floor, and she goes on manipulating her bow over the screaming strings with so little effort and sounding like the virtuoso I know she is. She's got a grand future ahead of her, and Little Guy has me.

A Friend?

"So Devon, are you finished doing whatever important task it was that you were doing?"

"Lisha, what's going on? Need someone to carve? What, is your own skin all taken up, or something? You normally don't act so anxious to see me."

"Oh, get over it Devon. I guess I'm just bored, *God.* (fuck!) I'm chok—"

I can feel the fingers trying to go into my mouth, my throat, flicking the teeth on the way. I can't talk anymore. (You're jealous that I am trying to spend time with someone else.) I gag, probably audibly, and hang up without saying good-bye.

And Where the Fuck Is Jenny?

I was her savior that day and now all of a sudden, she's

curiously absent. I haven't seen her for about two days now. Maybe she could take some of the pressure of them off of me. (You should be more appreciative that I didn't allow you to come out full force only to someday go back feebly as old gets. Are you looking for your mother? Will you do some of the same things to her? Will you start at the hole you came out of? Finger first, slowly at the edges, a light touch to awaken her? Will you then punch your way back in as you came out? Or will you start with a clutch—a pull—then a thrust? You don't want her to enjoy it, do you? Are you afraid she'll take it with pleasure?)

Age 10, Maybe

I need to help him dress still. I don't want him to have any accidents trying to get his insect-skinny leg in the pants ever again. There was this one time when he tried to do it himself, my Little Guy. He was exceptionally crafty that day, waited until my back was turned to get him an undershirt out of the drawer. All of a sudden I heard an unusual crash, unlike his typical, that is. I turned and saw Little Guy tangled up in a cocoon of hatred and corduroy pant legs. The look on his face was pure butterfly fury. That's when I knew. The fingers had probably intervened, yet again. (The *fuckers* that you are! Jealous bastards!) I quickly ran over and rescued him from the net, like the savior I am.

I've kept an extra close eye on him since then. Of course, like any kid, he doesn't want help. He mouths, *no!* He still doesn't talk, save for the occasional flutterances, due to his hatred of his own voice. I am constantly bemoaning the way it comes out verbally versus the brilliance that must be locked inside his brain.

The butterfly is slowly growing up palsied and without the freedom of the outdoors. The feathers on his wings are gone, destroyed by touch. The wings are gone. Twisted limbs have replaced them. Braces and metal plates have replaced the feathers. Grace has merged with fumbled ambulating and has left the equation of *this*. Fluttering has merged with the struggles. Life force tried to kill the fist and it is angry. It won't get the last word, though I, Lisha, *über* Aunt, will see to it. For if I don't, no one will, because everyone has forgotten about him. Why has everyone, including his mother, forgotten about him?

"Sculpture of Butterfly Child," Glass, Wire, Skin

I create a sculpture to destroy the fist for good this time. Its wings are an intricate design of broken glass fragments and tiny wire braces. I attach pieces of my own skin to it—some are bloody, some are burned; all are exquisite as only skin can be. These are pieces of me (you have pieces of me now. Essential to *you*, but my skin can grow back; this isn't *forever*).

I offer it. The fist grasps it and then it leaves me alone for a while, and goes straight to the middle of the closet straight under the light bulb and then it is gone, leaving a stain on the floor. (you are now, the way you were then, nothing more than a stain on the floor of the closet). Now we're equal.

I am part of that butterfly that the fingers have taken away.

Mother of Numb

enter and function girl you just gotta function just
smile your (numb) well-adjusted girl-smile and she'll
never know how you are feeling **normal** is the key to
this sewer-brain (*Numb One*) don't smile too much and
time will go by (numb as the hand after the wrist is
carved)

"Aunt Linda! Over here!" **sit** down or she'll think
you're standing too long

"Lisha, baby. Don't just stand there, give me a hug!
"**consume** you **touch** her flesh and think about touching her someday when she's lying in a coffin on display—"You're not sick, Lish, are you?"

"Nah, Linda, I'm cool." **sick** as the head on her
shoulders say it just like that see her reaction

"Want a cappuccino?"

"Are you having one?"

"Sure, I love them here. My treat."

"Uh, well, in that case, you want me to go get them?
I mean, like, it's the least I could do for a free mug o' joe."

"Sure, Lish, I could handle sitting down and staying
off my feet." **she's** pregnant and the baby is dying its
death will truly and inevitably happen and will hurt
her like kindness but she should thank the gods for the
experience it could grow up a Viking girl like you or
weak fairy girl doomed to the happy normal (as numb)
life can she know you love her **you smile** the child
doesn't matter **you are functioning**

"Can I help you?" says the counter boy.

"Yeah, two large cappuccinos. One extra strong." so you can beat his **candied** fucking **brains** in with no effort

"Right away. That's four dollars, 25 cents, for you, beautiful. Hey, and smile!" (**die**) "Things aren't so bad! I bet you look gorgeous with a smile on your face." **no,** actually, you look gorgeous when wielding some sort of weapon preferably on yourself

"Whatever. Here's five. No, keep it." **use** it hopefully to go towards some sort of recreational drug heroin maybe and it can be his first time and like he'll shoot a blank die like a bitch without even getting the benefit of the high first

"Thanks! Hey, and smile!"

"Here you go, Linda. God, I need the caffeine buzz, man."

"Don't I know it. Baby and all." **not** the baby stop no no don't think of *that* **but seriously** caffeine could do some major damage it could be born totally stoked and hungry right away for the brain tease don't think that it will be a healthy child it will be a healthy child brains and all **or** maybe a **shell baby** sometimes babies are born without brains those they kill right away and chalk it up to a casualty of birthing the baby is just cartilage now could probably play some mean fucking smear the baby across the floor games with it **what** would she say if I said this to her right now

"So, how's it going kid?" **don't** be cruel don't be so cruel (numb, numb is the key)

"Oh, just fucking dandy. School's a breeze as usual. And dealing fine with *her*, husband and all. He's not such a bad guy, actually. Keeps the hell outta my way, that is, you know what I mean? Heh heh." **smiling** is a good thing right about now

"Look, Lisha, I called you for a reason. I think we need to talk."

"Oh, yeah? I know, it's been a while. Too bad my mother couldn't be decent and invite her only sister to her fucking wedding, for Christ's sake. I mean, it would have been tolerable if you came."

"But she didn't want that. That's okay, I can respect her wishes. I've come to realize, reconciliation just isn't going to happen any time soon. Lish, maybe it's time you realized that too. But that's not why I wanted to see you." No to admire your scars **faded** to pale

"So, out with it, Linda." **you** grin and expect the world of light to ebb away into a galaxy full of hell and all its dreamy creatures

"It's you, Lisha. You, sitting here, smiling at me, acting so calm and unaffected. I heard about the wedding from Aunt Kay. She was worried about you, frankly, and I can see why. You don't even talk like usual." **like a Viking Girl** "I thought you were okay, that she had to be over-reacting like a typical old lady, but I can see she wasn't. (numb numb numb numb, numb numb numb numb, **none**, none) Getting suspended from school, running off with your boyfriend, I could almost deal with because I knew you were coping in your own way. The scars, the razor stuff—*this* I don't know." **you** see flashes of silver like a soldier just stepped on a land mine in the 'Nam **now** shrapnel in your insides, perhaps

"Like, what do you want from me, woman? I'm *dealing*, okay?"

"*Dealing?* I don't think so. I'm not equipped to handle this, Lisha. I can admit that." **oh yeah** and she dies like a baby dies easy and faintly so pretty **lily baby** the ephemeral flower her baby is **wanted** so not like a fist can someone want it sometimes

"So, deal how? I'm cool, I tell you, like drop it, 'k?" **baby** flutter butter flutter inside flutter baby dies with just a touch **escape** to numbland before anyone can see you and becomes attached

"The bottom line, Lish, call this number. It's for teenagers going through rough times." **rough** how would she look **no** how would she react if you took that straightedge blade you hide from time to time under your tongue to use on designs at random how would she react if you gave her a design on her **motherly** face and would it leave a scar for her baby to look at while sucking on her tit **pretty designs** you're talking flowers with long vines and large fertile buds for the bugs to feed upon you're talking toddlerhood childhood and even adulthood the scars would fade to pale but always there for baby to see

"Look, Aunt Linda, it's nice you care, really, but soon it'll be over and done with anyway. I don't need a phone number. You know us kids. We get over things..." **orchestra** of blade violins and knife cellos hammer drums all to kill the audience of listeners and smoldering incense to create a mood "I'm hanging in there! I won't disappoint you!" **grin** corn syrup-sick

"I only say this because I care, you know that Lish." **blades** (caring creating numb) and babies grinning **razor-empty** grins born brain-free blade-free burning sludge baby grin **grin** grin because you're happy

"I know you do. But hey, there's no need to worry. I promise. Haven't I always told you everything? I can

talk to you, like you're my big sister or mother or something, only you know better than that, because like,
you've treated me better than she ever did." **whore** she
a garden whore lying there letting some dude fuck her
and implant an incipient flower and like it **treat** it like
an act of god "So, don't worry about me." **can stare** and
see it through the clothes and skin and all to baby
curled so much like a fist but this one isn't it's *wanted* a
flower that won't be burned **dead-brown** by the evil
light bulb

"No, I'm just going to sit here and nod and believe
it's all right like everyone else wants to, yeah. That's
what you expect?" **expectant** garden-variety whore
spreading her legs and swallowing the splurge of flesh
with her homey reception between them "I'm going to
be a mother, for god's sake, and I hope to hell I don't
become like a *typical* mother. You think I'm so far from
you now, don't you?"

"No." **you** yourself far from you now you **don't
want** this "I'm sorry. I'll tell the truth. I can't deal with
that *mother* any more. She can't deal with me. It all
sucks now, okay? I only stick around because Jenny's
there. She's all that matters." **pregnant face** her pregnant face caring you want to rip it open like a perfectly
wrapped Xmas present with deliciously bad brains
inside it

"*Jenny*? Lisha, my God, will you just stop this? You
know she's *not* there."

"And what the hell do you know Linda? Just what
the hell do *you* know? Jenny is, Jenny is—"

"No, not Jenny. *You*. Will you just *listen* for a
minute? Shut up for a *minute* at least. You need to hear
this. Okay, God knows, your mother wasn't easy deal-

ing with even when I was growing up. She was six years older and all but I couldn't handle it, you know? I was glad that she went away to that religious school when she did, even though I knew that it couldn't last. I used to overhear our mother's friends whisper things like, 'That girl just isn't right.' It was weird to hear all that being said about her, to know her and wonder where the hell she came from."

"*Isn't right*? You don't even know—"

"Oh, yeah, *I* don't ? Look, I had a time of it growing up. But I'm through with blaming her because this kind of thing, fuck, it can't be helped. It's all in her head. Do you get this? Does it make sense?" **you see** the train coming you see the headlights you see a child sailing out in front of it and the whole thing is so slow **so magical** so beautiful better than an amusement park ride or virtual reality strobe lights disco ball baby creating colors on the tracks and you watch it all fixation reads your face (numb like the wrist)

"Lish?"

"What are you telling me now. That all along my mother is fucked in the head? Now that's propitious, all right. And I should, like, *understand* her? Try to understand her? What does that have to do with me? Oh, something insipid like 'love conquers all,' or something *special* like that. What the hell should I understand?"

"Understand you're not so different from *her*. Yeah, there's a shocker. You don't deal with things the same way, but those thoughts running through your head, I know what they probably are. Want to know why? *She* thought the same damn things. I heard her talking. She used to do some things that seemed funny to me, but I was just a kid. I accepted the strangeness of Christine because what the hell did I know? She wasn't hurting me in any way, just herself, I guess. But there was something so exciting about her. I remember when she was pregnant with you—those nuns sent her back home and god, did she beg for an abortion at first. Our mom was religious though, and that was out of the question. She would cry that you were *chomping* on her insides. Mom sent her to talk to the priest, cuz that's the only way she could handle it. Christine was quiet for a while after that, but then the other stuff started. She was completely obsessed with giving birth, even said you were the second messiah born to a virgin. I remember how she would pray out loud in her room. She would still complain about the pain in her womb, but she accepted it like it was her due. She seemed, I don't know, ecstatic or something when she'd feel you throbbing around in there. Then you were born. I was so happy for her then, I thought it might even make her almost normal, but over the past few years I could see your mother... maybe..."

"Yeah?" **mother** this is mother calling

"Maybe she shouldn't have been allowed to even have you. She kept saying all these strange things when you were born, how you were the final sign of the Apocalypse and shit. Mom decided to keep you and send her back to the convent school, so she could get this stuff out of her head. It didn't really work, though, and whenever she'd come home she would start in again. I would look at you, trying to find out what made you so "holy." That was the end of her short career as a nun, or however you choose to call it. Though I guess she's still getting maximum mileage out of that experience. Mom argued with Chris to let her raise you but she wouldn't hear of it. Even I knew at that time, it would have been the right thing to do. But she insisted she was a grown-up and more than capable of being a parent. She was determined, and took you away and so..." **sighing** her air coming from her lungs collapsing like pup tents collapsing around her words (numb collapses around) baby replaces amniotic fluid in the sac and you have to expel yourself the fuck out of here

"I really don't feel like hearing this, okay, Linda? Look tell me when your child comes, I gotta bail." **run** move function go through this crowd of contented cemented expressions crowded over steaming paper cups steaming around faces like gases **poisonous** gases get the fuck out the haze damages kills makes disfigured nuclear move move move

And you can dimly hear, *Lisha wait! Lisha, don't leave like this! Lisha, come back! I'm not finished!* But she is.

V.D. Hearts

So RAZOR SLASHES HAVE FADED to light purple scratches, so you're practically ugly and just plain again and need the designs. Coffee burns—red marks like kiss marks, hickies but sweeter—up and down the arms and you think of getting some boiling water later because purple and red do look so good together, so good, like a loving couple on a V.D. prevention ad.

V.D. kisses hearts and promises—oh happy V.D.—just you and your scars to share, to fuck...Billy?

Pour the boiling water into shapes of lips puckered in kisses, heart shapes, little on the arms, large on the chest or stomach to collage with the purple marks so meaningful and better than Godiva heart box of wicked chocolates. True beauty, true love exists only in pain. You want to make it real and so satisfying (pins can make more accurate hearts). Don't forget the pretty orange-red coils of the stove, just begging to be used, I slightly lean, and the design is already there, swirly perfection.

Candles burn to add atmosphere to the romantic aura. You and your self-torture—no not torture never but love, a love no more fucked than yours and Billy's. The only love you want—the only love you need—the love of the blade—the wick—the stick—the pins—the flame—the bleed—the weapons—the bugs crawling (millions of crazy cockatoo bugs, black with red feathers—they're crawling through the hearts—crawling—

making disgusting arrows of their own).

Bugs warp all the perfection, but this is *you* working, Mother of Numb.

The Phone Call

I have to call him. It's been ages, but he must need me. Our love. He ruined it with that bullshit with Jenny. I think it's fine time for some major "fuck with him" payback. I guess I miss him.

"Hello?" Innocent boy voice. Innocent as the mythical horny rodent.

"Yeah. Billy?" I've gone girl now.

"Who's this?"

"You *know* who."

"No, trust me, I don't."

What a dolt. I'd love to fuck the daylights out of him now. It's the boy voice. Then we could, of course, engage in some mutual body harm. Just like old times.

"It's me, asshole. *Sweetie*," I add as an afterthought.

"Lisha?" He can't disguise the delight he feels!

"Yeah. Listen, uh, we gotta talk."

"Lish, what the hell changed your mind? I mean, not too long ago, you came over and freaked me out with that shit—"

"That bit of fetus, your *fetus*, and don't you forget it *honey bunch* of love."

"Whatever. So what the fuck has changed? What's up? You want to shove some other crap in my face, or something?"

"No, actually, I think it's time to get back together," I sing upwards, slowly seeing the hearts burning—evaporating from my skin to the ceiling.

"What?"

"I said, I think it's time we get back together. I'm bored with all of these other dorks I've been seeing. I've decided to forgive you and all."

He doesn't say anything right away. He must be stunned and ecstatic both. I understand because it is rather magnanimous of me.

"You couldn't help yourself. It's a boy thing. You were young. I understand."

"But I didn't ever *do* anything. You're fucking crazy, Lisha. Like, you say, your *sister* gets pregnant and you come over here screaming like some kinda banshee or something about me, uh, *fisting* someone named *Jenny.*"

"No, man, get it straight. That was *your* fist you made when you fucked *my sister*, okay?" *And Man Created FIST.*

"Your sister...what the fuck? Then you don't talk to me for a few weeks, except to give me the death stare in the hallways or completely ignore me. Of course I'm not gonna even try and talk to you when you get like that. It's like you're psycho. And all this *after* you fucking came in my room late one night presenting this bloody thing wrapped in a towel and saying it's my *fist*—"

"You should have seen your face," I chuckle softly.

"Yeah, real fucking funny." He sounds pissed. But I can remedy that.

"Awww. Billy. I'm sorry. But you know how important my sister is to me. You should have seen the pain she had to go through for that." My voice is flat as a pre-silicone chest.

"But what the hell does that have to do with me? Just because one day your crazy head tells you I got your sister pregnant, I have to put up with this shit? Listen, just leave me the fuck alone, okay? God only knows what your fucking head will tell you next."

"Billy, are you insinuating that I'm a luuuunatic or something? How sweet of you. Come on, come over... *Baby*," I add for good measure.

"For what? You're one fucking *crazy* chick. I didn't completely believe it even after we did that road trip, but I know now, okay? Just keep the hell away from me, okay."

He's so delicious when he's mad! I know it's just that anger thing talking. He still loves me.

"Okay, you want to know what for? I'll tell you," I deliciously draw out the words like pieces of caramel. "I am all alone in this house right now—no fist, no sister, no Nunny. Just me, lying on my bed, talking on the phone and getting hornier by the minute. You dig?"

He's real quiet. His dick thinks for him. Doesn't it always?

"Lish, God, why do you gotta be this way?"

"Just don't forget the razor blades on the way over, I'm all out. *Baby*."

"Lish—"

"Just don't forget. Oh, and by the way—"

"What the fuck else?"

"My sister is dead. I can tell you this now, though I guess you already know anyway. But this is fucking *important*. I've come to some sort of understanding. We'll talk later, sweet one, buh-bye."

I hear his exclamation as I hang up the phone. Joyfully.

Lisha Has Billy 4ever

He came to me before, and now he's sleeping in the fetal position, such a puppy, right next to me in my bed. I play with the jelled blood on his arm and luckily there's enough of it to script, "Lisha has Billy 4ever" on his arm, gooey like cake gel being squeezed out a tad messily from a tube onto white frosting. Blood is sweet. A Valentine cake, of sorts. I sink again into my pillow and think of things as I fall into a semi-sleep.

Billy...he crept into my house, into my room, like an alley-boy in black; frightened, sleek and stealthy, gracefully cautious, so perfect standing there for a second staring at my body, naked and scarred fresh for the occasion. Scarred fresh by the burns and pin pricks, all for love. He produced a slim plastic case of blades and handed them to me like they were jewels for my approval. I sat up, lotus-style, set for the ritualistic romance.

You're so beautiful, he told me as I cut myself anew with a perfect diamond, cut a perfect jewel onto my wrist, a tennis bracelet of rubies, because diamonds are sharp, but rubies are more beautiful because of the rich red they color onto the flesh. He found his way next to me and I felt his cool, moist breath tainted by toothpaste, first on my face, then stinging the fresh cut on my wrists.

Me, too, he breathed in my ear. I did, and then we're engaged. I didn't say anything, because I didn't have to. The sound of sharp instrument on soft surface invaded the dead silence of the room. I didn't have music on. The magic was music to my ears. The cuts are magic. I love Billy.

You didn't ever fuck my sister, did you, I finally murmured after making my mark. *No*, he said, sobbing, finally, and buried his head into my breasts. *I don't get it?*

They never do. They never could. And then, the next hour was divided between sex and the real *lovemaking*—the union of blood and blade. We both took our time. And then he fell asleep. And now so do I.

The fingers, the fist, Jenny. All are gone and it's like they never were even here in the first place. Billy's back.

I rule.

List of Recent Accomplishments In the Infinitive

TO DRESS UP, TO DECORATE, to prepare. Jenny. For all.

To beautify. My skin. And the others'.

To create. With blades.

To singe. The sea with exploding watermelons pregnant with explosives. My mother's hair, tacky making big.

To save. The innocent fish. Devon from getting involved with too many people contained in one person. The children. Little guy butterfly.

To trip. Surrounded by tall trees. On I-95. Teasing Billy.

To protect. The children by warning them with real-life fairy tales.

To help. Jenny and her fist. Jenny from her fist. Her fist from the stale air of the closet, the burning light bulb.

To rake. A garden with an aberrant flower. The fist. The fist as flower.

To play. Xavier and his brain. Nick and his several pieces of...

To display, to imagine, to make new. A wedding resplendent in decay: roses, daisies, fabric of gauze and tulle. Festival of children posing as the dead. An Angelica just for me.

To D.I.Y. Do it yourself. Depend on yourself. Fuck others and their various respective baggage. Destroy a fist. D.I.Y. Die.

To hallucinate. Reality. What is really happening all around me.

To realize. Hallucinations are in fact reality.

three: Now

WINTER/SPRING 1989

*And now...the aftermath
and all its rosy implications...*

The Newest and Most Bizarre Disciple

"DEVON, HAVE YOU EVER THOUGHT…"

"Oh, yeah, it happens all the time."

"Come on, cut it out. This is serious, man. Have you ever thought you saw or, I don't know, *felt* a ghost or something."

"You know, Lisha, yeah, now that I think of it. That time after I saw *Amityville Horror*, and then went by the house on Ocean Avenue to check it out, and yeah, I looked in those spooky-ass windows, and yeah, like I definitely saw a ghost. I think it appeared like red smoke, or something."

"Yeah right, and you had been tripping right before, so don't even try to hand me that line of bullshit, *Christ*, can you be fucking real for like, even a goddamned *minute?*"

"Well, Nick says he sees them all of the time—"

"Nick? You call that being serious?"

"Okay, fine, Lisha, no, I never saw a ghost for real or anything. What's your point?"

"Oh, fuck it. I'm bored—can you get your mom's car, do you think?"

"Where do you wanna go?"

"The mall. I need to feel superior to others for a little while, at least."

"Okay, Lish, now what the hell are you talking about?"

"It's *Prom Time*, boys and girls."

I walk past that bastion of people protecting stores, different faces—same paltry brain matter and I look up at the glass mall ceiling to stare at the sun pouring like piss over the heads of the consumer trash. They are, of course, oblivious, walking into Chess King or The Limited or Macy's.

I want a blade. I'm overwhelmed by a compulsion to convert one of the mall masses. There are lots of girls around my age on shopping sprees to buy their prom attire. *Woo hoo.* I want to find someone who may be buying a dress of chiffon in *Baby Blue in the Face* or *Lick Me All Over Lavender* or even *Prick Me Pink* for that matter.

"Come on, girlfriend, off to Orange Julius!" Devon doesn't even try to pretend she has any brains. *Orange Julius*, indeed!

"And what the fuck am I going to eat there? Please tell me."

"Oops! (Giggle) Sorry. Nick and I always eat there when we come to the mall, so it was automatic. How about the yogurt place?"

"Nah. I'm not even sure hunger is an issue at this point. Look, you go over to the big, greasy OJ and pig out. Go on, be beautiful. I need to go buy something and then I'll meet up with you in there, though I'll probably barf as soon as I cross the threshold of that food graveyard."

"Uh, okay." She's asking for it by giggling again.

I will find *The One*, I have no doubt. This is a test of the magnitude of my influence. She cannot be from my school, or else she'll be predestined to an opinion as soon as I approach her. This is a pure, untainted mind that I am after...

I enter Macy's, where the dressing rooms are partially communal. I grab a bland dress in *Give Me Green Dreams of Post-Nuclear Landscape* and go inside, all prepared to stalk my girl. I hear a nasal, "Ma, come *on*, no, I'm no size 12. Get me a different size ten in fuchsia, damn it."

Ma storms out totally frustrated and doesn't even bother shutting the door, so I peer in and see a genuine Long Island Debbie in her stall oozing out of the seams of her *Fuck Me Fuchsia* tea-length frock. She's a blonde beast busting out of the size 12, but not for long. Blood makes beauty. Her skin is virgin.

"Hey, girl!" I startle another roll of fat to pop out of the neckline.

"Eeeew!" She gives me a quick, disparaging once-over. "What the hell do you want, freak girl? Halloween is months away." She laughs like it's the funniest thing she has ever heard.

"Okay, first lesson. That is a cliché that I could smell coming from a mile away." I make a point of sizing her up. "You're really quite fat, you know. A Gunne Sax nightmare, should you choose one of those bright McClinctock frocks. Therefore, fuck the fuchsia and go for a more flattering *Graveyard Dirt Black*. It's almost like science to figure out the right prom dress color. Get it?"

She's just standing there, more fat popping out of the top of the scalloped neckline like a bubbling brook, on her face a show of outraged party girl with shit on her nose.

"Ah, yes. *That*, my precious, is the difference between a clichéd insult and a brightly original commentary that is an insult buried in the context of a constructive criticism. Get it, deary? Now, I'm actually not here to insult you, or anything."

"Look, my mother is coming back in a minute, so just get out of here, okay? *Weirdo!*"

"Come come. You know she won't offer you any solutions to your dilemma. Why not get dressed quick, ditch the dresses and come with me? You can't go wrong."

"Why would I want to do that? The all-black thing is so 1983. You look like a witch or something."

"And what more do you need? You need some kind of spell to get out of this hole."

She'll never know that what I'm after is Island-wide ubiquity. Long Island is a big place full of half-wits begging for conversion. This one will be a challenge, what with her wannabe Debbie Gibson ass, but let's face it: it gets boring converting those already converted.

"Eew. Look, just get out of here." She looks like she just swallowed a wad.

"Look, *missy,*" I hiss as I grab her pudgy arm, so smooth and clean I want to vomit, "I'll play you this way, dig? Okay. All of these dresses are meant for the lithe teenage girl body, not *yours.*" I change my tone to cream her with kindness when the fear dances in her eyes. "You're more than that. You have the body of a *grown-up woman,* yes, be proud! (That's what Oprah would say to her hefty teenage guests with low self-esteem.) I *wish* my body would hurry up and look as mature and ready for woman things as yours is now. But the fact remains, you won't look good in one of these prom dresses. Better move upstairs to where they make dresses for the *mature* woman. The styles are more sensible of course." I can see the wheels turning in her head. One thing's for sure, she wants to fit in one of these teen dreams.

"I don't want one of them ol' farty dresses. *Gross!*"

"Well, come on," I say in my kind and sensible voice, "You admit you need my help, then."

She stands in the middle of the dressing room looking like one of those ballet hippos in *Fantasia,* and catches a glimpse of herself in the three-way mirror. She stares for about a minute and bites her lip. She must instantly regret those midnight 7-11 and Taco Bell rendezvous. She looks utterly defeated.

"I still look fine in my kick line uniform, you know."

I've won. I just smile sympathetically and nod.

"And I'm going to the prom with Joe Capalone. He's the quarterback for the Massapequa Mustangs."

"Wow, a nice *big* football player. They have to go out with someone substantial, now. No skinny little girls for them," I add as she looks like she wants to kill.

Just then her mother walks in and looks at me suspiciously.

"Is this one of your friends from school, dear?"

I can tell she ain't so happy about that.

"Look," she says, "I chose one of these in a nice navy blue from the Ladies Department upstairs. I think a dark color that's a little more *simple* would be more flattering to your figure, dear. Ruffles are just too busy."

"Mom, just forget it, okay? And go. I'll take the friggin' bus home."

"But honey, I thought this was something we'd do together! I have an eye for this sort of thing. You need my help. This is our *prom.* God forbid you choose the wrong dress..."

"I don't need anything from you, Mom. Just go home! *Gawd!*" She wails the god part.

"Fine, just don't come crying to me when you pick out something you'll end up hating. And pick something that fits you right, for heaven's sake. I won't have a repeat of last year's Junior prom fiasco, going to a dress maker to let it out for an extra hundred bucks so you could fit into a size 9. When are you going to accept that you're full-figured?"

"Get the hell out of here, Mom!"

"Fine, how are you paying for it, smarty?"

"With the credit card I took out of your bag, *Mother*," she spits.

And Mother storms out of Macy's.

"Debbie, how much time until your prom?" I say casually.

"It's this weekend, why?" Yep. At her wits' end. Last chance. Perfect.

"Well, I have a way for you to lose some quick weight and you don't have to diet or exercise."

"How? And whatta you think, *you're* so hot? Nice hair. What did you do, use a magic marker to color those strips? And it's so flat. Ever hear of hair spray?" She laughs at what must be, in her eyes, my "bumpkin" status.

"Now, now, there's no need for that. Unfortunately, everyone can't have that Long Island status symbol of big hair. You don't see me spending my nights alone, though. That's what I'm trying to tell you. You have to overcome those commonly held misconceptions of beauty. Do you know who I am?"

"No," she snorts. "Should I? You can't possibly be in the *Group*. What school do you go to?"

That *Group* to which she refers is what is commonly known amongst Long Island high school kids as the "cool" people. That is, jocks, rich kids, cheerleaders, and anyone else deemed by the preceding assholes as cool. Cool by association counts some too.

"Honey, I go to Westend School for the Arts, and the *Group* you hold in such high esteem is begging to get an appointment with me. I just don't have time to see all of them. Besides, they're just a small part of my Master Plan."

"What the hell are you talking about? *Master Plan?*"

Bring me the dense ones.

"You'll see. Are you coming or not?"

Oh, she's coming all right. She just cannot resist the lure of Lisha.

Metamorphosis

"So, what's the big ol' secret, that I had to come over to your dumb house?"

"Let me just grab that tape over there on the night-stand, okay?"

"I only like New Kids On the Block right now. I'm sure I'm not into *your* kinda shit." She laughs.

"It's not that kind of tape. It's words. The words of others."

"Jeez, you are wee-ud!"

I present a small photograph to Debbie. She looks impressed. It's just some dopey cheerleader who begged me to do a design on her, but as I've said time and time again, I won't *do* cheerleaders. She makes an adequate model in this case, though.

"Oh, my *gawd!* She's so gorgeous! What did you do to her?"

"It's a secret. But she was pretty hideous before I got to her." I go over and press the tape recorder.

"Lisha, you have changed my life forever! I made captain of the team and every guy on the squad is begging me for dates (giggle giggle)."

This one, of course, I had to get Devon to improvise in the event of an occasion just like this falling into my lap.

"Okay, ya got my curiosity, what do you do?"

"It's skin designing, and I am the master. And don't you forget it."

"Skin designing? What does *that* mean?"

"Well, that depends on who I'm dealing with. For you, *darling*, it means that I will cut the gristle right the fuck off you. How's that for fast and effective?"

"Cut the—*what?!*" And she gets up quickly, presumably to leave.

"Just think," I say casually, "no dieting. No exhaustive painful exercising. That gorgeous Gunne Sax is yours, baby." I can't even say *Gunne Sax* without wincing just a little.

"But that's gotta *kill!* You are fuckin' crazy."

"Not at all. For instance, I have my own type of anesthesia. Take five Percodan with three shots of any booze and you won't feel a thing. Of course, I'm just posing this to you as an option. You could just walk out that door right now and go back to the sensible *women's* section at Marvy Macy's."

"But this will mean I'll have ugly scars on my arms and then I'll have to wear long sleeves! I wanted to go strapless. Well, I guess I *could* just choose that bitchin' Zum Zum gown. It has long sleeves. It's backless!"

I'm still reeling from the fact she could be so banal as to say *ugly scars* to now gag at the Zum Zum reference.

And *Bitchin.'* Hello? 1982 Valley calling. They want their spew back.

So I'm just standing there, bored with her vacuous chatter, and suddenly I hear the words, "Well, whadda I gotta lose, anyway? The prom is only one week away." Success is like vodka-spiked ambrosia.

"Okay, but first we have to prepare you and the room," I say.

"Prepare? Like they do when they do liposuction?"

She actually just gave me an idea. Hell, I was going to just cut her the fuck up and not worry about the clean-up! Then again, there would undoubtedly be more waste with this one.

"Oh, yeah, that reminds me to go get the vacuum. It's a cute little number. It'll minimize the mess and I can quickly suck up the fatty goods. But what I actually meant by *prepare* was to light some candles, burn some incense. And play some music. Mood is extremely important here. Needless to say, a NKOTB tape would probably melt in my player, so that's way out of the question. But I have a demo tape from a band that my best friend's psychotic boyfriend is in. They're not too bad. Loud is key." Masks the screaming pretty well.

Everything is all set. I give Debbie her "anesthesia" and she's pretty fucking out of it. I, of course, would never go near such a thing when I am doing my designing. I can appreciate it enough to imbibe at other times. The only thing is, she's singing some stupid pop song.

"I get lost in your eyes..." she sings in a maudlin soprano.

Could it possibly have come to this?

So I take a new blade, sharp and sweet as a well-sucked lollipop—that sweet—so sharp—and hold it up to the candle to make sure it is sterile. I couldn't deal with a lawsuit if I gave her some dangerous infection. And I absolutely refuse to ever go to jail. As I bring it close to her upper arm where the flab is most prominent, she stops singing and looks a bit apprehensive. I am inspired.

"Just go on singing your Debbie Gibson, darling," I coo and lightly touch the blade to the areas I plan to target.

"It's our prom song!" she sighs.

Next, I take a majick marker and draw lines, like any plastic surgeon would do. But my marks are made with style. Might as well make it appear as "authentic" as possible to her, without compromising my art.

"I get weak."

And I make the final preparations to slice into her right then. That song fires my ire like no amount of poisonous gas ever could. I take that blade, so shiny I can see myself in it—my eyes, concentrating, victorious, content. Never wavering. The glance takes mere seconds and I am ready to use—to abuse—to ravish this girl's skin. Fat is deeper than I've ever gone before, though.

Slice slice, better than the most exquisite torte layers of skin bloody icing. So deep, such makeup, the garbage of this glimmer girl. Her fat—I envision it gleaming when it comes out. Happy to be freed from its prison of skin. Eager to die without its barrier.

Her eyes are glazed, but gleaming still gleaming in the gloaming lit with candle light. She's waiting.

I make the first cut. I feel that rush when I hear the familiar swoosh of sharp blade on soft adolescent girl skin. Pearls and rubies of blood. Tiny, then growing larger and larger. Fragrant. Precious. Yes, even hers.

"You *go*, girl! You totally fucking *rock!!*" I shout as I take the nozzle of the mini-vac and put it at the cut, so like a slit of mouth and I'm sucking up what is vital to the make-up of this Little Debbie girl. There's an obnoxious slurping sound, but Debbie is too fucked up to care, if she even notices.

What I'm actually sucking up is the *figurative* fat that is her make-up. By taking that out, she'll be like a totally new, *worthy to be alive and sucking up precious air*, person. It may not amount to much, to the eye, that is, but to her psyche, well, that's all that matters. *And beauty will crowd her flesh like buzzards.* And the gorgeous scars, though not traditional designs per se, will be beyond conventional standards of anything.

True beauty, I say over and over again to myself. *Alter the skin. Alter the make-up and I will make a new person. True beauty. I see the fat evaporate into millions of question marks that speak "why" to me in a silent chorus of pained exhilaration. The fat doesn't know. The skin remains, marked by these slits which are a bit more gaping than anyone's I have ever done before.*

I repeat the same action on her other arm, her back, her thighs. No need to venture elsewhere at this point. And there's just no way I am approaching her ass. That's *her* problem. It's not like she can see that anyway, and that's what the Jane Fonda tapes are for. Some things you just have to work on.

After I finish, I stand back. She's totally passed out by now, the combination of pills scotch intense pain thought. She's like the prodigal bride of blood, a fucked-with mermaid, lying back on the chair like she's out of the water and can't survive. She's beautiful.

I have to clean up, but not too much because the vacuum cleaner was pretty handy in that respect. Next I'll put on the gauze as well as the ceremonial glitter bandages before she can observe her new look. Just hope the blood doesn't seep through them, as there is an abundance of it still streaming out. Blood is beauty, true, but I doubt Debbie can handle such unconventional beauty at this point.

Metamorphosis Complete: Several Hours Later

She wakes up and sees me staring intensely at her. Check: eyes filmy as webbed cocoons, mouth a tad ajar, waiting for brain to connect to word, face a rose garden; her soft skin surrounds the bandages, and underneath, I can only *dream* the possibilities.

"You're ravishing," I say. I wish now *I* were fat. She doesn't say anything. She seems dazed by the pain. Well, I did think she was kind of weak, but I know it's more than that, because I've had that feeling. She's under the influence of a celestial pain. I bring over a full-length mirror. I see my image behind her; she is superimposed onto me. I shudder and we become separate again.

"You can see how you look, but the bandages can't come off for another day. It's a must," I add.

She doesn't respond. Just stares at her mummified reflection. It seems as though everything visible is bandaged except her face which is still intact, anyway.

"You know, I fucking hate those losers, NKOTB," are her first words, forced out. *It worked.* "Fuck Debbie Gibson and Tiffany!" She looks deep into her eyes in the reflection.

"Ooh, I look amazing!" She breathes. Indeed, she looks at least a pound lighter, and even if the scale doesn't show a big loss, well that's probably because she's retaining water. That's what I'll tell her anyway.

She looks at herself from every angle possible. Perception is everything. Besides, the metamorphosis is so much more than the superficial appearance.

"So, will it be the backless Gunne Sax?" I ask fearfully.

"Nah, Gunne Sax bites, man. I want to get a hot number from Long Island Trash, on Hempstead Turnpike. That's like the new LI version of St. Mark's Place clothing stores."

Okay, what I want to know is how she figured that out after only one design session? It must be something paranormal, this skin thing. It even made me look at myself differently in the beginning. She has definitely changed, and for the better. *For the better*. For starters, she smoothes down her big Aqua-dolphin-Net hair and grabs my purple glitter lipstick.

"I can't wait to get off this fuckin' stifling Island."

"Uh, I know exactly what you mean."

"What I mean is, everyone on this fuckin' island all think they are so cool, but they're just a bunch of fucking posers. I can't wait to go to the prom and do some serious annihilation. It's like I owe them or something. But first thing, grab me the phone, will you? I gotta cancel my date with that loser from the football team. *Joey*, ugh, what was I thinking? Jocks are so *vacuous*, and it's not like I need him or anything. I gotta be strong. There is no "we" in this game of pain, right, Lish?"

"Huh?!" How the hell did she know that? She couldn't

have heard me say that. Was she privy to my mind during the process?

"Uh, I'll get the phone." I give it to her and she stabs at the numbers.

"Hello? *Joe*, is that you, *Dear Heart?* Listen, I've decided you *bite* and I'm going to the prom alone, you dig...Well, *fuck you*, 'cause I'm not fat anymore, you'll see. Trust me, *Babycakes*," and she slams the phone down.

I sense something bad. Transformation is cool, but this is just too uncomfortable.

"They're all gonna *freak* when they see me at the prom. I mean, how hardcore can you get? This is really *me*, Lisha. How did you do this?"

"Just all the majick girlfriend," I uneasily chirp. At this point, even I'm surprised at this big hair chick getting into my shit.

"Well, this is just the beginning. Trust me, it's gonna be *big*, girl, you can count on it."

"Big, how?" I ask.

"I don't know. A new world order, perhaps. Isn't that what you wanted?"

"Uh, not, exactly. My plans were somewhat smaller scale. Think underground ubiquity. I don't need the masses to embrace me. That is *not* and never will be my thing. Where's the perversity in that?" I will disagree with anything at this point.

"To hell with being perverted. I'm talking about opening people's eyes like you did for me."

"Oh, why bother with that, I mean, fuck people, that's what I always say. You were different. Sort of an experiment, if you will. It's not like I want a bunch of people following just for the sake of following. To be cool. Ugh. Come on, Debs, think, *think!*"

"Look, what the hell do I care if you agree with me or not? I'm on my own now, thank you very much. I appreciate what you've done for me and all, but in the end, it'll just be me, right?"

"Uhh—" but that is so not true, especially in her fragile case. She's so new. I mean, even I had my come-uppance via the fingers.

"Before I go, though, I'm gonna raid your closet. You don't mind, do you?"

So she does need me. She is speaking *my* mind, *my* thoughts, but words are not actions. She's not even getting it. Just what the hell is this Debbie? She's in the closet and I wait for her to leave.

Yet Another "Unveiling"

It's the next day, and I have to be present for the cere-monial removal of the bandages. We are seated in front of the mirror yet again. She is so jumpy and jubilant, tattered and trippy, sardonic and savvy. Fuck.

Debs definitely is not her own creation. At first, I thought, how could it hurt to let her glom some of my stuff. A secret thrill to see this chubby mummy raiding my wardrobe of vintage rags yesterday. What she picked out was the fine decrepit frock I wore for Nunny's wedding. Of course it didn't exactly fit her, but I allowed her to do what she needed to it, not likely *I* would be wearing it again.

However, I was a little surprised to see her with the same hairdo as mine. Late last night, she came over begging me to take off the bandages, I thought, but really to show me something else.

"Knock knock!" I heard in a brightly sarcastic tone, not unlike my own. I immediately looked up and saw this Debbie, but it was not Debbie anymore because her hair was *mine*. Platinum and Rose Red.

"What the fuck did you do?" I couldn't even think of keeping my cool at a time like this. I mean, my hairstyle is my own.

"Oh, just got tired of the 'do. Whaddya think? Isn't it cool?"

"Cool? It's *mine! My* hair. Get it? What do you think this is, like a goddamned cheerleading squad, 'follow the leader?' My hair is not a trend."

"I don't know what you're talking about," she said airily, ignoring everything I just said. "Now, let's talk makeup!"

I did not delight in seeing this former Gunne Sax gal wearing a blonde bob with two red stripes in the front. She did this without my permission, for Christ's sake. But could I kill her?

Ahh, the hell with it. She has to undertake my mission now, so I can't abandon her at this point. Afterwards, on the other hand, well, I can't be responsible. Fuck her then.

But now, now it's time to see if the magic took place. That's the important thing here, the thing I can't allow myself to forget.

"Okay, Debs, are you ready?"

"Oh, I'm ready all right. You rule, girlfriend."

"Stop saying that!"

"Huh?"

"Oh, just forget it already. Here we go."

First I take off the gauze off her back. Even I have

to admit this job is beyond perfection! Some scabs have formed on the incisions, and they are, as always, valuable jewels.

"Oooo eeeee!" She squeals. Whatever. I quickly follow with the gauze around her thighs. More of the same perfection. But when I go to the bandages on the arms, I realize I am the True Visionary.

"Now, would you just feast your eyes on *that*, Debs!"

We look together and we both see. The tops of her arms are a message to me, and there is no denying it, but I want to. The cuts are in the forms of fingers, five on each arm, the perfect five. And as I look, as we look, the fingers' formations change into different signals.

"What do they mean?" breathes Deb, as mesmerized as I. They flutter, they speak in their finger language. I do not know it. I do not want to know it, but they force me to see.

Debbie is you, Debbie is you, you'll see. This is the fingers' mocking salute. I can't get away from them. They want to leap right off Debbie's skin.

"They are a part of you," I realize aloud. I am stunned. "Are you real?"

"What the hell are you talking about, girlfriend?"

"You're part of the ruse. You're a—" I back away from her, this wraith of fingers now. She is not a girl, but a device.

"What the fuck ARE you?!" I shriek. "What the fuck ARE you?! Get the hell out of my house!" She grins at me, triumphant, as the fingers surely are, takes the tip of her forefinger and touches it to the design on her arm. They merge and become one another, and her other nine fingers soon follow.

"I am Debbie, not Lisha, but I will become more

than Lisha ever could. Off to my event, my OPENING, if you will." She flounces out of the room, not before grabbing one of my vintage frocks and then slithers out. And she takes the fingers with her.

But I have it in my power to control her, so I will do what I have to. She's my puppet, fingers or no. I have to think, I have to act, I have to tap my resources and the only way I can go is to think, it'll happen at the prom. It'll all come down there. I will not take it easy on her, for how do I know what the fuck she is? The fingers think they can come back and win, but she is my creation. *Mine.*

The Debbie Doll

She and *they* just think they have won. But no one realizes I have the pieces left over from her. I usually don't dispose of such things by way of the garbage, but save any left over bits of skin in a plastic baggie. Then comes the ritual burning in the closet. This is what I planned to do with Debbie, who lost so much more of her makeup, what with being so bovine. There's stuff in the mini vac, which is still on the floor by the mirror.

Sure enough, I have located the pieces of Debbie and so this will not be the end of it.

I'm on my own now, she said. She cannot even think original thoughts.

I gather the pieces for my work, the handmade Debbie Doll. There's the stuffing (plenty), the hair (big), and the clothes (deliciously *gauche* as only a Long Islander's could be). And her skin. I attach the pieces to my newest sculpture, in this case, a doll. A slashed arm here, a design there, the stuffing leaking. I color it red, but not with my blood, as she is *not* me. I do it the hard way, find her leftovers, dried now, but I wet what I find on the towels and make do. Her doll is more beautiful than she is, more than she ever was.

And then there's the setting I must construct so that it will all be so perfect. The gym with its ridiculous decorations, the fellow students dressed in their prom wear. I will control everything. Lisha is in control, folks, don't worry. I still have plans and they will take effect on prom night. She is *not* me.

And now the prom process is to begin. I intend to be more than a vicarious participant.

Debbie Does Prom Night

DEBBIE DOES ME.

She walks into the gym, intent on her new world order. *Listen to me.*

She slips past the Ticket Geek at the door, biting off and shouting, "tickies here!" He's so full of himself.

The gym vomits its decorations down the childrens' throats. "Under the Sea." Millions of girls in aquamarine and boys in tails, begging to be drowned. Debs has the saucy gleam in her blackened eye. Other girls, in dead-baby colors, yes, those pinks, blues, lavenders and yellows, all avoid her. *Listen to me.*

But no, she goes over to those who shun her the most and just stares tidal waves at their faces.

"Look at me now, baby, just look at me now. Look, loook…" She wails like a sea siren would (always fitting in with the theme). They laugh, uneasily at first. They are scared of this sea siren, this fucked-with mermaid. Never you doubt. My creation.

There's football Joey just a few feet away, Debs. You go to him. You go girl. I can't resist.

"What the fuck…" he stammers.

"Don't you wish I would have let you take me to the prom now," she asks dreamily.

Oh yeah, you're his wet-dream girl, you know it. Go ahead, drape that cut-up arm around his big shoulder. He's strong.

"Uh, how'd that happen?" He's uneasy.

Use that Debs.

"What the hell happened to you?" His date, pretty in putrid pink, turns with a smug look at Debs, which quickly turns to roaring red horror.

"This," and she whips out a blade with a flourish. *But hold on, that's not my cue yet. You'll ruin it.*

"Come here, Joey, stud boy," she murmurs.

Too soon, She-spawn? Go slow. Take it easy. You have to win them over first. Put it away like a nice girl.

"Get the fuck away from me, Debbie. Are you nuts?"

"Get back here."

And she's out of my control now. She's way the fuck past me. How could this happen?? I can only watch and see my powers free of my constraints; they've taken on a life of their own. And lo, and behold, *the fingers are back.* They force me to watch...they wish me to pay. It's their game now.

Debs, how could you? Try being selective, for God's sake. You're so indiscriminate with your blade. Using it on those who are totally unworthy. This is what sickens me more than anything. Choose the special ones. But no, there you go, disgustingly out of control, slashing about like some jock with a marker making a banner.

The children are running. This girl has gone completely Carrie on their asses. But here it is 15 years later, and the dresses did not get any better, despite losing the overall hideous style of the '70s.

AND SHE SPIES A FAT GIRL. She'd been looking happy all along, out of Deb's range. She looks content in her Spot Me–Swim Me Aquamarine Dream. No use in ruining complete complacency. What's the point? And Debbie (she's out of my control. The concept of "you" is lost, forgotten and buried) gets all on her case, especially when she freaks at the sight of the wielded blade.

"Your loss, lard ass!" She screams when the girl doesn't want to lose some of the flab by the all-curing razor blade. It's like, fat is cool with her. Why get on her case? Debs *wanted* to change, after all. Who could resist assisting her when hearing that whiny voice in the Macy's dressing room? There was some subliminal begging going on. Why blame *me?*

Why are they back???

Why are they back? Why are they trying to choke me? This isn't my fault, can't they see? The fingers are through with that game and are back, fucking my throat and if I was there, in the shoe box prom setting, I'd be the new circus geek, grabbing at my throat like it's a chicken's neck after I bit the head off.

Not me, I say, I think, to them.

The Girl Children (They, Like Me)

IT'S 8:30 A.M. HOMEROOM. Girl children with colored scars. Beauty—the designing of the skin—like me: girl children—fingernails split from the scratching, like me. Girl children eating chalk and licking eraser crumbs (crumb by charcoal-tasting crumb) off the desks, like me. They all want to be me. I don't want them to. Let them eat paste instead, I beg. I realize eraser crumbs smell like burning skin.

Okay, so. Be me. Just for a moment of finger torture and choke. Just for 1/4 of an hour of tickle and hair pull-out. For the eyeballs gouged. I look all hard, but I'm soft enough for the probe of the fingers to find what's vulnerable and oozing. That's right! My skin is *soft*. Soft and yielding as a baby's fontanel. And there's nothing to fuck today because this little girl is too soft to hold painful penetration. Don't think I miss it, because I'd rather have the hardness to catch the punch and never flinch. I become full of holes instead.

8:45 a.m. First period. Walking down the hall, I see the followers of others walking and there's no beginning to the crowd. I am full of holes, too vulnerable and bulimic to pass by a bathroom that could prevent me from embarrassment. All full of holes and the other girls' smile?! The fingers cooperate by fondling my tonsils, and I retch breakfast product on their Nine West foot wear. They are horrified, but still embrace me, asking, *Are you okay, Lisha?* They must want something from me. They must want designs cut into their nacreous-pink girl skin.

The stench quickly permeates the hallways and the girls retch just like I did mere seconds ago. Is there any end to their emulation? They want pink sunshine and yellow frost. Shades of blue to color everything rosy and new.

The boys don't exist in the hallway now, because they are weak and full of confusion. They exist in person, but don't matter until there is an ounce of sweet recognition in their brains and dicks. As of yet there are no such candies.

The fingers don't leave. They will never bother to reach the boys. Nor will they be fooled by the *perceived* superficiality of the girls, either. Only *I'm* their target of probe and succulent pain. I want it to stop, but what will I be doing with my hands for such an extended amount of time if I am not constantly thwarting (or attempting to thwart at least) their 5-finger orifice assault? Carving designs into skin! The fingers must resent me for that pleasure.

They want to be me. At least three girls hide their slight swell of baby under large sweaters and bemoan fabricated tales of "porking out." I know better, though. Why would anybody want to go to the closet *on purpose?*

They want to be me. Until there is no me anymore. I started this to see what would happen and now I'm almost overwhelmed by the implications. Shall I succumb to the fingers of the fist? I just saw a girl who carved her face of her own volition, and I was not consulted. It was a bastardized version of *face.* I'd never do the face. There's enough implicit variety of character supplied by the eyes alone. One needs to voyage her blade onto the bland landscape of the torso and various appendages. If she had the brains to consult me first, I would have saved her from needless hours of "concerned adults." After all, you can't clothe the face. It is naked and vulnerable and a bizarre work of art in its own right. *There is no sleeve for the face.*

They want to be me? Why? What would Jenny say to that? Would she instruct her baby fist to punch me in the face for inspiring an island of girls to Lishahood?

But no! She can't be behind the fist. *That* fist. *Her* fist as it came to be. Once it became free it was out of her power. I won't allow myself the comfortable thought that Jenny has the opportunity for revenge. That's too easy. The fingers are of that freed fist. The selfish, wanting to be "alive," fist, freed from the closet. An entirely separate entity from my beloved.

Do these little girls know of the invisible rakes carefully placed so that I step on them unknowingly, and receive the full-blown fury of the stick hitting my forehead? That is, every time I forge ahead quickly to leave the flowered fist and its fingers behind. It is all the more clever for never seeing the light save for that of the closet. It's almost as though I am all of the world it is ever going to experience and it wants to make everything out of this small facet of life. I have no choice but to withstand its life force.

Maybe I should thank it. Maybe I was getting too self-absorbed and self-important. Jenny is gone and the fingers are forcing me out of my comfortable land of make-believe. They are forcing me out by the throat. They are forcing me out by the eyeballs. They are forcing my organs out to the evil atmosphere and then sucking them back inside to the humid body. Every inch of myself has been made aware. I should thank them, yet I can't get *through* to them.

They want to be me??? Then let them see. Let these girls perform their own helpful acts resulting in misery. I will be their catalyst. I will not say no, but I don't encourage. I don't even need to. One must learn her own threshold of pain, herself.

They want to be me? I can only guide them to the closet.

Choke

ALONE ON MY BED, FACE DOWN so that the fingers can't get my eyes. Knock on the door.

"Yeah?"

"Lisha, are you coming to eat out with Greg and me or not? We're going to Red Lobster. I'm sure they have something without meat."

I can't answer. I squeak.

"Lisha? Come on, it'll do you some good to get out of there. Meet us at the car."

Maybe the fingers won't bother me if people are in close proximity. Like family. Only problem: apparently the fingers see themselves as my family now.

I fight (*them. I fight them every inch of the way...gagging, forcing breath, battling the force that tries to blind me like sugar in my eyes*) my way over to the closet to grab a tattered black shirt to cover my arms—I'm in no mood for the expressions of suburban-ites. I make it out the door before I realize what I'm about to do. Red Lobster.

Her face brightens like a flare for some reason.

"It'll be nice, Lish."

"Yeah, whatever," I mumble and head straight to the car. The fingers haven't made it there yet. Mom and Greg get in the front. Greg doesn't say anything. She's chirping non-stop like a cicada.

"Linda told me she spoke to you the other day," she starts excitedly. I don't even want to deal with this right now. "I think we're going to try and patch things up a bit, you know."

Don't do me any favors, I wish I can say, but I'm afraid to open my mouth for fear I'll be choked.

"I think it's time. You'll never be closer to anyone than your sister, right, Lish?"

How the hell could this bitch be saying this to me now? Is her specialty torture gardening, or what? I'm so weak, I can't even prevent the tears from forming in my eyes. I try to look pissed instead, but she can still see the tears. Maybe it makes her uncomfortable, so she turns around and starts fumbling with the radio dials. Greg's turn to be a parent.

"Lish, I guess your prom is coming up. You and that guy, what the hell's his name, Bobby, going? Man, I remember my prom," he chuckles like he has some arcane knowledge.

I just glare out of the window. I can't help myself, though. "Yeah, actually we are going. I was even almost at one the other night to assist a friend in her attack on the student bodies. Wanna hear about it? Or maybe you should turn on 1010 WINS and hear the news. Although I think it's more meaningful to get the news from the source itself."

"Lisha, what are you talking about now? Can't we just go and have a nice dinner?" She sounds tired. What a pity. I just got my second wind and am not about to waste this opportunity to use my acerbic wit.

"Sure, lets! I agree! Why the hell not?!"

But it's like they heard. They are fighting for first dibs in the speaking hole under my nose. And the long nails, they make use of themselves by drilling cavities into my teeth.

"Lisha, I am begging you not to be difficult tonight."
She turns around again and is satisfied when I don't
answer (*I can't*) and takes this for my consent. It's so
easy to mistake silence for peace.

They keep turning the torture on and off.

At Red Lobster I make it fine to the table. I'm practically whisked in, for Christ's sake. The three of us are
seated as the almighty "family" at a huge brown fake
wood table. The fingers are probably amused. Remission? The tacky menu has cartoons of happy lobsters
and clams, as though they just *thrive* on being eaten by
greedy Long Islanders.

"Hi! My name is Missy and I'll be your server tonight.
What appetizers can I get for ya?" She is so peppy that I
have to cough from the wind escaping her orifices.

"Well, like, hi *Missy!*" I squeal. "So glad to be your
master today! What cheap deals can you get for us
tonight so that we have money left over for a tip?" I
mirror her bright smile. Her fingerless countenance.

"Are you all ready to order then?" This is said in a
lower octave. Her face mildews just slightly, like the
first fuzz on a cut avocado. We all give in our orders
and Missy leaves.

"Lisha, that wasn't very nice. Just let the girl do
her job for God's sake..."

"Nice? You want *nice*, OK tell her to get her ass
back here and I'll show her nice just fine—" And I am
choking, so I grab a glass of water to wash out the fingers.

"Please, just calm down! Why does every thing have
to be an event with you, Lisha? Let's just eat in peace."

Greg just sits there, not saying anything, looking at
his utensils. I'd like to know, why is it all about peace?
And does she even know the meaning of the word?

She starts conversing with Greg and I feel I should retreat to some sort of children's table. Finally, the food arrives. I guess I'm a little bit hungry by now, so I dig in my bowl of linguine with plain marinara sauce and stuff in a forkfull as unladylike as possible.

But it's time to pay. They start with the long, skinny pasta, wrapping it around my neck, so that the sauce resembles blood and the pasta a mess of naked nerves at first glance. Suckage of breath from Mom who begins choking on some piece of seafood. Greggy leaps up like some sort of savior, but then looks over at me angrily, "Can't you eat like a normal fucking human being?" I'm trying! I want to say, but cannot. Cannot swallow, cannot breathe. I just want to vomit what I could have swallowed by now, but I can't even do that. The vomit lies waiting to erupt from my esophagus, burning like biled lava. Marinara is tough. I feel like a serpent out of a lagoon. I feel like a frog about to burst with blood and guts. I feel like a tortured viola, over plucked and bowed. My throat is full of fingers, pasta and piercing sauce.

And finally the fingers have their finale, the *pièce de résistance*, in adagio. My throat is suddenly free of blockage and I fall to the ground, hands at my throat. I explode into vibrato and look into the circle of obnoxious instruments in front of me. They have strings and sauce all over their faces. I fade into a different orchestra, but not before glimpsing disgust on specific faces: Missy the perky all-Americana, Mom, and Greg. *And my torturers, they are doing it with glee. I am being moved somewhere else. I go willingly. It's not like I have a choice.*

A Fairytale Existence

WHITE STERILITY. My first thought is virginal, soon to be replaced with smut to color the walls gray. I smell the old and ill. I smell weakness. I have arrived here in this body, in this enlightened room of the dead, dying, not dead. I. Am. Not. Dead. I am aware. My jaw aches like too much bubble gum, dick jobs, or whatever else was forced down my throat—jaw likely pried open while they pumped me free of pasta and fingers. They are gone, aren't they?

"She's awake!" The best words I've heard all night. My scope widens to take in the room in its gestalt. I see ducks and chicks on the walls. Rebirth or just a mockery of myself as being worthy of such a thing?

"Where are they?" I can speak, rather croak, now.

"We're here, honey." I look over to the source. I see my mother and her husband. Not them. *Them.* Why can I think this so clearly, yet not articulate it?

"Noooooo," is all I can get out before I'm interrupted by some sort of caretaker. I could detect even the slightest glare at this sensitive point. But wouldn't anyone if they were constantly being attacked. She wears the white trash white uniform.

"There there. Don't you go talking too much. Your throat is quite raw right now. Just rest your voice and eat some Jell-O."

Rest the voice, but the brain is still so active. MY JAW?! And what about *my jaw?*

Jell-O. I can't even imagine voicing my distaste of eating a product that is sweet enough to disguise the animal hooves. The Devil's food. Sensing movement, I look towards the doorway. I see a familiar girl floating by in a hospital gown. Nursey follows my gaze.

"Know her, do you? But, then, how could you? She came by several times to look in on you this evening, I noticed."

I'm somewhat shocked, but then I realize she must be one of my followers.

I hear the nurse whisper to Mom about a shame or something, "Young girls today...the new and unconscionable method of disposing of a baby...an epidemic...fourth one this week. But we try to be empathetic here. It's for the courts to decide."

She thinks I'm responsible for this. In fact they all must be thinking it. I know. My tally reads this girl, Jenny, and a slew of others. Lisha, the girl responsible for a generation of closet children.

I want to explain. I want them to know this wasn't intentional, but I'm immobile, starting to drift off again into the bayou of the unconscious.

I can feel my mother holding my hand, squeezing it—and then all those in the room concentrate hard on the beauty of my arms. Their eyes don't hold the designs in any esteem. In fact, my mother leaves the room, choking. The nurse clicks her tongue and Greggy runs after his beloved weak white flower, browned around the edges, just beginning to decay.

"Well, look here, now. You have to see Dr. Kahn for sure. Self-injurious behavior is cause for psychiatric intervention."

Well, psycho, huh. You try to feel the ice of the

shower's spray into a fresh cut and tell me that isn't the best fucking feeling in the world. But I can't say a damn thing. Her face looms above me like a fleshy water balloon, spreading, spreading, getting bigger and bigger...

I can't feel them and for a moment, I mistake their absence for mercy. Only when I open my eyes again do I realize they were in temporary remission and are now about to put on a show in the tradition of the Grand Guignol.

I see that girl from the hallway again. She approaches me smiling, as guileless as a puppy. She sits down next to me on the bed and I realize who she is. Angelica? I never knew I went to high school with her.

"I did it! Now I'm just like you, but not as hardcore I guess. I waited until I went through labor and only then did I throw it out. Hearing that pitiful screaming almost did me in, but then I thought of what a favor I was actually doing it."

"Angelica, but you were a child."

"Yeah, ten years ago, maybe. I'm a mother now. Or was," she chuckles.

"Lisha, let's go, honey. We have to run tests." I wake up to those chicks and bunnies on the walls. Why are they invading my room? I've woken up to innocence, though just a guise. Nursey to my right. Nervous Mom at the foot of the bed.

"Mom! I..." Can't finish.

"Now, now, stop talking! Come on! You must save your voice. You've been through a lot. Talking is the least of your worries." Nursey chuckles.

I have a feeling she is in on it with the fingers. Perhaps she is their flesh and blood agent. In fact, I'm certain of it.

And what *have* I been through? A bad meal at Red Lobster? I look over at my mother who is trying to smile at me. Trying not to look like a flustered woman with excess Woolworth baggage.

WOMAN. That's what your beloved Christ called his mother. Don't make me call you "Nunny" again. I shake my head and try to get up out of the bed. Nursey thinks she's being gentle, holding me down this way. I bite the bitch. Hard.

I feel a prick in my arm and fade away, seeing my mother's face full of chagrin and her mouth form angry words to Nursey. It's *them.*

It's them, I want to shout, but the dark is too comfortable to leave. I feel the scratchy bedsheets underneath me, yet I exist in some sort of "otherworld." How soft it could be, existing in two places. I smell burning sugar, cotton candy, and then I see pink. The paint of a little girl's room? It's one of my kiddie's rooms. I can't speak, but I think really hard. I still cannot remember her name. "Psst! It's me! Your Viking Girl. Things aren't too cool, you know. Hey, my girl, how's about helping me now? I helped you once, remember? That was cool, right? I'm not cool. I'm sick from something right now. And I don't even know what it is. I think it's a real fairy-tale this time." But the form turns and it's not the girl I thought it was. It's the fingers in a brilliant girlish disguise. And they all come at me. I turn and run. I run down the pink cotton tunnel, the candy like the insulation one may use in their attic—the one with the Pink Panther on the wrapping. It is endless until I notice a break in the fuzziness and enter. Here it is dark as fuchsia. I see boys jerking off to the walls and their cum is pink; I want to go lick it up to see if it tastes pink as well. But fooled again! They're not boys, they're really fingers. I didn't know they were capable of morphing, of multiplying that way. No, I can't believe it. I must stop them, not to run—that's the pussy way out, fingers can break, can't they? Suddenly the fuzz is gone and I see all is still pink, but it's not candy anymore. It's skin now. Pink nacreous skin. Razor-less, I want to rip into it with my nails, but ever quick to the challenge, the fingers have pulled off my nails and all I am left with is mushy weak skin and blood at the tips. The cruelest gesture: I look at them and see their nails have grown to amazing proportions, which they do not hesitate to shove in my face as I wail with the wall sirens. I guess there is no way out.

Why have they brought me here? It's not dark enough. The dark is easier on the soul than the light. Why are they torturing me with the bright pink light? And now, an intense dreary golden light ramming down my eyes.

So bright, this light bulb. There are tears, eager to save my eyeballs from drying up.

"She's with us again," the bland male voice says. I automatically sit straight up, unable to help myself. I can't talk. I can only breathe.

"She'll be just fine, ma'am." Now, why am I being referred to in the third person? Talk to *me*.

"I...Am...Here..." I get out with great difficulty.

No one looks at me. The man with a white jacket takes Mom by the elbow. Why is he so gentle with her? And then, the muffled tones, which I could hear just fine. What the fuck do these people think, I'm some kind of invalid? I try to get out of the bed again.

"Do you see why now we had to medicate her earlier?"

"But doctor, that nurse jabbed her just because she tried to get up. She wasn't even trying to be nice about it. Just jabbed her and made her go to sleep."

"Ma'am, that's what she needed, I assure you. We have to do this when the patient seems to be a danger to herself or to others. She is enduring some sort of painful feelings that are just too much for her. This may be the cause for the psychotic episode."

Mom starts to sob, out of control. So ladylike. Call the priest, folks. Absolve this girl from her sinful thoughts and actions. I snort. I still can feel my throat, raspy.

"Waaatterr..." If I could just make my throat feel better before I am attacked again.

"We try to do our best with our kids, ma'am. You may just have to face this and get help," says he.

"Here, honey."

I try to swallow, but gag.

"The parents are often the last to know, believe me ma'am. Nothing is conclusive yet. We can treat chemical imbalances with various medications. There are many new developments in the antidepressants."

If only he could break away from his precious medical gems for just a moment so I could know what the fuck is going on!

"But believe me, doctor, I've been there myself, so it's not like I don't know what you're talking about. Before everything happened, she was acting like her old self."

"Why don't you describe her behavior to me? It could help me. I am, after all, just meeting Lisha's case right now." How would my behavior *help him*, a fucking stranger?

"I don't know. Quiet. Sullen. And she got mad when I asked her too many questions. She much preferred keeping to herself."

"Ma'am, this behavior combined with the self-injurious behavior, is maladaptive indeed. Recreational drugs are a strong possibility. She was probably taking them due to her depression. The 'black dog.' Believe me, it is not an unusual phenomena with today's teenagers. Did she break up with a boyfriend, recently? Girls typically over-react in cases like these."

"Jenny did not have anything to do with that!" I don't know where that came from. They all stop talking and look at me.

"Tell him. *Tell him.*"

"Who is this 'Jenny' she speaks of?" the doctor says quizzically, like I'm a specimen and not really there or something.

"*Tell him!*"

But she hesitates.

"Jenny was her sister," Mom says reluctantly. Then she whispers in his ear, but I hear what she says.

"There never was a Jenny."

Doc's eyes grow large like he's struck gold.

"Of course," he nods viciously. "Let's go to my office, ma'am. We can discuss more there. Don't you feel better about this now?"

Huh? I find my voice in the face of such oppression.

"Hey, I'm still here, medical slaves! Here! Wrapped in white. Cute as a slug in a bed. Made of melted Silly

Putty and Color Forms, all plastic." But they leave and don't come back. Then Billy and Devon come in.

They approach the bed like I'm already toe-tagged.

"Hey, I hear death can be a real ice-breaker," I try. They just look at each other.

"Hi, Lish."

"Billy! Can you believe this? One minute enjoying a festive meal at Red Lobster, the next hooked up to syrup in a bag. Check it out. Like the tube is a huge Pixie Stick pouring the tangy syrup to the joy of my veins. Heh."

He just smiles lopsidedly, like a jack-o'-lantern carved wrong and left by the radiator.

"What up, *baby?*" I say to remind him who's the Viking here. Only it comes out like I'm the Viking's captive babe or something vile like that.

"Lisha, your mom told us what happened." Devon, ever the Spam Queen, so mushy and formless and disguised by spice.

"Oh?" Gotta play it cool. How did they find out while I had to contend with the fingers? And why the fuck can't I know what is really going on?

"You know, you're my best friend!"

"And you're my girlfriend!" says Billy.

Sort of. Is that on again?

"My *darlings*, I don't have amnesia, you know." They look nervously at each other.

"But…" Devon chews her lip.

"Oh, fuck it. What do I have anyway?"

"You don't know?"

"Truth be told, no, I don't. I just woke up a little while ago. All I keep hearing is medical propaganda.

Goddamn it!"

"Whoa! After two days of what, being in a coma or something! Holy shit!" Billy starts pacing the room like an expectant father to the alien birth of bitch.

"No, more like two days of being on *muchos drogas*," Devon giggles.

"WILL SOMEONE TELL ME WHAT THE FUCK IS GOING ON?"

"Okay, girlfriend. You were in Red Lobster enjoying an immense bowl of pasta when you started clutching your throat and gargling some freaky kind of words or something. Some guy thought you were choking on an artichoke or something, so he began doing the Heimlich thing, but you weren't choking. Just kept saying something about hands grabbing you and then you passed out, not before making a huge scene. Oooh, lucky, Lisha. They have all the cute buff waiters there. They probably wanted to save you, take you into their big, muscular..."

"Cut the shit, Devon. Get on with it."

"So an ambulance came. They did tests on you and realized there was nothing uh, physically wrong with you, uh and, uh brought you here to get better."

"Uh, where's here? I mean it's the hospital, isn't it?"

"Uh, no. Well, here is...uh, let me put it like this, Nick was here once! Now you guys have something in common!"

I AM. CRAZY?!

By the way, Billy is way out of the room by now. Boys are such pussies when it comes to issues like pregnancy and insanity.

"What the fuck are you trying to tell me? I'm gonna waste away in the loony bin? I'm getting the fuck outta here, *now* man." I pull the IV candy transmitter out of my arm and jump out of the bed. "I thought I was physically ill. Now this all makes sense! No wonder everything was all hush-hush. If they think they're gonna make a frontal lobe-less Francis Farmer or fried Sylvia Plath burger out of this glimmer girl they're the crazy ones, not me! I am getting out!"

By the time I'm at the closet to get my coat, a nurse and another guy in scrubs walk in and gently (as if there could be such a thing here) escort me back to the bed. I fight them, but it's no use. I'm wearing slippers and my feet slide all over the floor as they hold my arms.

"Devon! Call my aunt Linda. Help me get the fuck out of here, okay?"

They try to push me down, but I am too strong to succumb.

You all leave me alone when I'm the strong bitch, don't you? The strong Viking Girl, huh? Maybe I want to be here again. I want to settle things now, once and for all. My heart feels like it's just a blurred image, and breathing is no easy trip down I-95. You think you've got me by the throat, don't you? Well, I've got a shocker for you. You're my creation, and not the other way around. Don't you forget it. So I'm back in Fingerland. And I can deal just fine. You all can come at me. At this point I have nothing to lose.

Before you begin, I want to tell you a story. A Viking Tale, my specialty, you know? Note the "you" in this equation. I'm not talking about some unknown all-powerful deity of "they" anymore. I'm right at you, now. I'm made of thick, hard rubber, my children. Note the "my" here. Yes, you're mine. Mine Valentines, mine little ones. But let me begin.

Once upon a time, there was this girl. She was a teen born of a teenage nun. Of course she was raised Catholic, for mum the nun couldn't deal with the guilt either. Teenagers are lust automobiles, made up of sharp but luscious stained glass windshields, stained by blood and bodily fluids, with just a little skin thrown in for good measure. Why can't anyone accept that?

One day this girl suddenly had a sister. She loved her sister. They were the proverbial "best friends." Oh they did many fine things together, but there wasn't any money for toys, so these girls had to "make their own fun." When they were little, they'd play for hours in the dirt garden out back. I say "dirt garden," for there were stunted yellow flowers—just weeds, really—back there, and nothing else. The neighbors would stare at them and whisper as these girls sprayed water into the dirt and bathed in the mud. They craved the nutrients in mud, so they would indulge in the occasional mud pie. The older girl wanted it so bad, she just dove in one day and then the younger girl, intrigued by the grainy drool seeping out of the corners out of her sister's mouth, so like a filthy vampire girl, begged for a taste. And the older one obliged, however the younger one didn't appreciate such nutrients and began to throw up. The older girl began to cry, but whispered, "Come on. Be strong. Love the dirt. Love it. Crave it."

Years later, the girls became their own sorts of lustmobiles apart from their mother. They were way past playing in the garden out back and wanted boys to play with. And so they did sometimes.

It was the Fourth of July when the younger girl went to the older girl for advice. And so she gave it. But not before experimenting with the fruit and discovering the answer. And realizing that such a predicament must run in the family, so why not blame the source. The original source, that is.

And the younger one agreed. They saw their childhood garden had transformed itself into her insides. This is where you were, YOU fuckers. I knew you were wrong then. I just knew you were never going to grow up, but become the finger petals of a stunted flower like the rest in the garden of dirt and dearth, because that was the tradition. And so I killed you.

It all comes back to skin. My map. My mode of transportation. My mission: to help the others. But then I got you. And I am here.

I dream and fantasize about violence. That's the prime method. Burst them open—all the wonderful things—and make them more splendid, big, beautiful and full of the bright light of power. This will rain down on what's left of humanity. The end.

I dream about YOU. Yes, you all, making your mocking salute. Yes I'm commander in chief now. I want to burst you open like those watermelons. And the pulp of your fist, the seeds of your bone, flying through the air and disappearing like my sanity supposedly did. But it's back now, my children. And now I must validate you.

I'm Awake, I state. I'm back in the bed. "I've figured it all out. It's over," I whisper. "I am ready to blow this joint."

There's a semi-circle of "power" around me. They'd better get the fuck out of my way. I have dealt with things my way. They don't say anything. They don't move. So I get out of the bed, only I am buckled in with straps of leather. Don't they know I won't take this.

"I will take this opportunity now to inform you that I am a vegetarian and will not allow these dead cow strips touching my body," I say calmly. They look surprised, like they were considering the validity of my statement. "What sort of archaic practice is this? What did you mental midgets think by strapping me in? This is America, buddy, I know my rights."

"Young lady, we have every reason to believe you will harm yourself as you have in the past. We have only your best interests at heart. Why don't you just remain calm, now."

What heart and where? I'd like to smell it. I'd like to taste it.

"I don't 'harm' myself, as you prosaically put it. But I won't discuss it with someone as obtuse as yourself, Doctor Strangelove, because you wouldn't get it. My art—don't even bother to interpret it. It would be like President Reagan trying to explain the brilliance of Artaud. Go back to your reindeer games, doctor. But unchain me first."

"No, I'm afraid I cannot do that just yet."

My mother is hiding behind him. Eyes wide, like she's witnessed a sighting of the Blessed Mother.

"Mom? I have the answers now, trust me. *Tell him* I have the answers. I have exorcised the fingers. Tell him! They don't exist anymore. I have to find other ways, see? Art is forever changing forms, and I must have time to find a new one. Tell him, Mom."

"Oh, Lish," she starts feebly and runs out of the room like a cowardly rodent.

"You have been falling in and out of consciousness, and thrashing about terribly. What happens if you fall asleep again? This way you won't be a danger to yourself. Your mother knows we are just helping you. Please don't resist us. Trust me. It'd be better if you could just rest up, sleep is often the best medicine."

I know the game. I don't say anything. I just close my eyes and wait. They want me to lose it. I just have to get out of here, and I know that obeying like a docile sheep may be the way out. Then he shoots me up but I am ready to take it now—to enjoy it—I am

On The Island of Clouded Elsewhere

I survived the hurricane. I made it here. An antique tropical garden without the sun left to make it into a pernicious postcard of reality. The cool dark beauty of absent sunlight.

I walk over to the dark ocean and realize in the dimness that the water is a reddish purple. The sand is actually dried flowers, partially turned to powder.

I, as sun, bend down to touch, to torch, to scorch and just then I feel the small hand on my shoulder. I don't startle, for it's a kind hand. The first such hand I've felt in ages. The fingers don't torture with probe or caress. There is warmth, despite the lack of light. I look behind my shoulder and that's when I see her.

My Angelica, animated and pure, emptied of blood and therefore as ethereal as someone can ever get. Her skin is all the more clear for such a lack of blood and bodily fluids, which I see makes her a stained glass window there above her head. It tells a story of her childhood, what there was of it. She had a safe home and a gray bedroom full of warm things—furry stuffed Disney characters, gold plated trinkets and souvenirs, a tacky faded, false pink flamingo night-light, perhaps.

She still can't speak. She's a child, but an ancient one. Just look into the eyes. Those eyes which know all answers. I go over to search the depths of them as if they were the definitive eye, but she evaporates like a year of happy Sundays.

I am alone. Alone to feel the dry sea of violet petals and to hear the silence. Yet for a split second I hear something else. Perhaps a breeze that isn't a breeze swaying a palm that isn't a palm.

Am I in Mexico? Is this the Day of the Dead? And as I think it, so it becomes. I realize I am in a place that I can simply wish and BAM! I am there. Just to check it out, to make sure, I think "Venice" and see rat-infested palaces and smell the slime. I do not wish to close my eyes again. I don't want to lose the incredible beauty of glinting gold, yet I need to get back to Mexico. Day of the Dead. I am surrounded by vibrant skeletons.

The little skeletons can be my friends. Who needs people? I have enough skin of my own, a testament to my self-absorption, of course. One comes over, trotting joint-by-weathered-joint, slo-mo, to pinch my ankle with his ("he" because he is dressed like a he and for no other reason) bony fingers. No, it's not those fingers, but a skeleton-friendly set of five. The little guy won't stop grinning and then I realize, of course, that expression is frozen on his face. His little sombrero clashes with the sobriety of the situation. I find my voice and I say lovingly, "You're a dead motherfucker, my little one. Why the festive colors? I'd wear black if I were you, muchacho. Up for some of that killer Mexican gazpacho? You need some meat on those bones. Look out, here comes one of your clones!" A girl waitress comes over, walking, limbs disjointed, like she has clubfeet and fucked-up hips. Too many babies. She was probably out of shape once, too, that is, when she had flesh and skin. "Yo, girl, wanna wait on us? Where your babies at? Don't tell me, you got tired of feeding their hungry mouths and smashed them, SPLAT, against some wall. They try to suck your nipples off? This is the thanks you get my bony queen! Forget about it, just get me some ice cream." Of course she's all huffy now. This skeleton chick cannot take a simple joke. "Hell-O? Want a suggestion for use of some of that sass? Making scary faces at me, hey, I'll kick your bony ass! Let's go!" (Never fuck with a mother, I guess is the motto.)

As she's coming at me, I feel water, real water again. The sea. I am immersed in it. I am at the bottom of it, gazing pensively at the surface from beneath the surface, expectant. Waiting for what I know will be the explosion.

Teeny bubbles escape from between my lips in inky seeds, and all at once the sea becomes watermelon red and I am the explosion. Curiously, I remain intact, though, but see the fish-feeding possibilities of my sweet meat. I am left just the bones, skin feeding the fish.

I am a Day of the Dead doll like I always wanted to be! Lucky me. I test out my joints and am pleasantly surprised to find them quite flexible. Who needed the skin, anyway? I can play and play and play with the sand, not feeling, not breathing, just being. That's all a girl could want. But before I can satiate myself of this formless feast, this 'not feeling' fantasy, I am merely flesh-warm again, amongst the real and alive. I've been

Taken Out

By this girl. She touched my arm. She's touching it now,

tracing her long nailless fingers along my scars like they're Braille for "Life."

I move. I realize it's back. The skin is back. And I am not wet, nor is my skin dehydrated with powdery sea-salt. And she knows I am awake again. She starts like a good dream when you're falling dead from exhaustion. It's okay. I love this girl, I realize.

"Hey you!" I smile at her.

"Are you back? They drugging you too?" She is biting her bottom lip raw as she speaks. Or it could be from being "asleep," like me.

"Yeah." I yawn as I say this. "Honestly I'm not sure I mind. Well, I've found lots of great stuff," I say as I grin.

"Don't even joke about that. Do the mind-expanding on your own turf, and of your own choosing, understand?" She says this gently while patting her stomach searching for the kicks. I swallow.

"What's your name? I heard the nurse talking about you before."

"I'm 'Lucky.' Just call me that." She tensely smiles at me. "At least that's what they're constantly telling me here. I figured I might as well change my name."

"Uh, why?"

"Because my baby was born dead, so I can't be charged with murder by abandonment."

"And you did this to it because of…"

"No, Lisha, there is no 'reason' and there doesn't have to be any, right? That's just what they are trying to figure out. They see me as their responsibility now that the courts aren't touching it."

"No, I meant, yeah, you're lucky about that and all, but didn't you do this because of me?"

"Huh?"

"Wait," I say. "Don't you know me? Weren't you a part of the closet children? The Skin Kids? The Designers?"

"Well, I sort of know you. I saw you come in a couple of days ago and, uh, word gets around fast here. So, I kind of know your story."

"No, I mean from school. I thought you were in one of my classes."

"I don't think so. I mean, I go to Central Islip. Quite a ways from here."

"But you've heard of me over there, right?"

"Uh, no...what makes you think that? I heard you went to Westend School for the Arts. I don't actually know anyone who goes there."

"You were pregnant, that's why. It seems like everyone has been doing it lately. It has a lot to do with my power of influence. Okay, for example, how many kids in your school have skin carvings?"

"Skin carvings? I have no idea what you're talking about. Look, there isn't much time. Do you want out of here, or what? I have no idea why they're trying to keep you down like this. The stuff they're giving you...it sucks. Before you know it, your mother will not even object."

"Are you coming along, Lucky? I've gotta skip town after this one. Or else they'd probably bring me back in. I could use the company."

Who the hell do I have left to trust? Both of us are fist-free, after all. Nothing grabbing us from behind. Nothing making strawberry taffy out of our insides.

"I guess. I mean, hell yeah. Where will we go?" She is unsure. But I am sure enough for the both of us.

"You just get us the fuck outta here, girlfriend, and leave the rest up to me. Not too long ago I took a trip down I95 with my boyfriend. If it wasn't for some traffic violation, I would probably be sleeping on some beach under a palm right now instead of being in here. I hear New Orleans is a cool place to go. Why don't we head over there? Or somewhere close to Mexico. Texas?" I yawn with excitement.

"Hey, Lisha, you're not falling asleep again? Those drugs do a number on you. I can't do this alone."

"Nah, just give me a chance, not falling asleep at all..."

Back In the Closet

BACK IN A CLOSET LAND full of old kiddie shoes, note-books, makeup, dolls; and there I exist for what I expect to be the last time. I look around, and for sure, it's my closet, but larger. It's infinitely larger, maybe without borders at all. And there are dolls. Each doll has a per-sonality of her own, complete with commemorative stained glass windows above them. One is Lucky, but frozen with an expression of abandoning "mother" on her cloth face. *No, don't*, I try to say to her, and go over to comfort her, nurture her. Her expression changes minimally when I give her this. Her stained glass win-dow has her future child on it, an expression of love and devotion on its face, yes, loving her for her sacrifice. The window is colored red and purple. I want to examine the details closely, but then the other dolls clamor for my attention, too. Lisha, ever fair. Ever the healthier.

The Debs doll is bloated and frocked in faded vin-tage black. The dress is ill-fitting, and just is not her style, as much as she tries. Her arms are close to the real thing, but on closer examination of the cuts and splits along the sides, I notice the insides are hollow. I poke my finger into one of the cuts and feel the wetness on my finger. I taste this blood, made of grenadine. Of course she has false, sickly-sweet blood. On her face, confusion is mixed with deluded triumph. She is empty, after all. No stained glass window behind her; it is clear.

There are two boy dolls, side-by-side, arms tied in male bondage. One is psycho Nick, smugly full of spite. His leer asks me if I've fucked anything imaginary lately. *No, Nick*, I answer, *it's THEY who had been trying to fuck ME, only I've won, you see!* And the other boy doll is my sweet clueless Billy. Don't you know we were the end from the start? It was the easiest way to hate you, you see? Don't take it too personally. Think like you are an adult looking at us. *We're young. We'll find others.* I can't waste too much time thinking about it. You'll be on to your next black rags-wearing princess soon enough. Tease her like I teased you. Lick her all over for me. She'll be begging for more. Billy's stained glass window contains the trees of I-95, and cars exploded into glorious fits of fire.

Nunny doll, that's you, with your bleeding palms. I can still taste the cherry syrup. Fine, so I see you did the best that you could. What I hate is your learned helplessness, your *Oh, she must be sick, poor girl, it runs in the family*, attitude. You tried at first to argue with that doctor, but then you ran away from it, like everything else, behind God, Jesus and the Catholic Church. I guess priests are just men. You showed me that at an early age, so thank you. But THEY fucked YOU, and not the other way around, and there's the joke. Your blood leaves your palms and floats away to make a stained glass window behind you. This one is more abstract than the one on the windshield that time. The colors are vivid, the colors made from the real red blood.

And there's pregnant Aunt Linda right next to you, grudges forgotten like you promised, and she's still smiling like a new Mom. She's so proud of the glass infant in her arms. It doesn't ever move. It'll be perfect. Her window is pure and clear pearl, around the outlines, just like her past.

And next, my Angelica. You were real once. You were the true child. You died before your time. So your doll is as you should have been for so much longer. Your doll is a little girl, pure arms, no designs yet, for who knows if you would have ever gotten there. Maybe you would have been above that, instead finding your own original expression. You would have been a visionary of your times. I know that. You're wearing the outfit I found you in, white frilly "wedding" dress, black mary-janes. Not engraved or painted on by a well-meaning corpse designer. And your eyes are open. And you have a smile that was not forced upon you. Your doll is truly *alive* and worthy to be. Your stained glass window is not in the closet, of course, but back *in another place* that I've never been...

Little Guy Butterfly, you had potential. I see you as though you were born a normal child. But you're a frozen doll, because that never could have happened. You do have those wings, though. You're just about fully formed and out of the cocoon for good. There never were any body fluids to make a window after all.

Jenny? You *move*, unlike the others. You approach me. Maybe you're *all* the others too. Maybe even me. I tried to teach you. I tried to help you. Your death was only weakness, proving that we both had failed. You were there and then...you were a limp rag doll, wet from the crotch down. Your wetness, red, but not cherry syrup, though for a second you thought that's what it was. Do you remember touching it like it should be thicker and stickier than it actually was and then the

revolted confusion drowning your face, coloring it blue?
Why did your fist last so long after you? I hope that it
isn't haunting you now. *IT* wasn't because of *YOU*. You
were perfect, like a virtuoso's solo. You were dead so
fast. And now a stained glass mural above your doll,
made up of your face, so that I never forget. At its bottom, seven-day candles held by glasses embossed with
beseeching Christs looking up to Heaven for an answer,
burning women enjoying their travels in the flames,
and the peaceful Virgin Mary. Religion can become you,
like this.

So the closet metamorphoses into a garden. I'm in
that primordial garden yet again. A voice whispers into
my ear, don't you know, that's a woman thing? I retch
and up comes some mud, just like I gave Jenny that
muggy day so long ago, mud now appearing like haze
over the clarity of the garden. The fog keeps my
thoughts safe, but as soon as I think that, it disappears
and I see something at the very back of the garden. A
human form, huddled next to a rake. The form is
clutching that rake. I watch, under the spell of greens
and blues around me, above me, as this form slowly
maneuvers the rake towards its mouth and swallows
the wooden handle like a whore would a cock. I realize
that rake whore is me, as I come to, blasted the fuck
away from my fairytale.

Postscript

THERE IS ONLY ONE BED in my bedroom now, and I'm relaxing on it. The closet is across the room and I'm okay with it.

I still plan on going elsewhere. My 18th birthday is close and I'm not bound to stay here.

There has to be meaning in all of this. I'll let it find me. It always does.

Joi Brozek was born in Queens, New York, grew up on Long Island and moved to Manhattan to attend New York University as soon as she could. She holds an MFA from Brooklyn College. Published in a variety of small press literary zines, her other titles include *The Luckiest Girl*, *Georgie and Her Meat*, *The Porcelain God* (co-authored with Eve Rings, with whom she also co-edited Dirty Girls Press), *Blood and a Windshield Make Lovely Stained Glass* and *Strays In Pompeii*. Joi currently resides in Brooklyn where she is working on a new novel.